INTRODUCTION TO THIS HOLIDAY MYSTERY!

Santa's daughter is happily settling into her life as a baker. Could a fresh murder burn her biscuits?

Cindy Claus loves exploring the human world and baking amazing treats. She should be bubbling over when her aging landlord takes her under his wing and promises to leave her the bakery in his will. However, before she can stir up a celebration, her patron collapses, dead, like a bad soufflé.

With suspicion instantly falling on the budding baker, Cindy must rely on her fragile new friendships and her father's trusted arctic fox. She'll have to sidestep local law enforcement as she gathers crumbs, and one wrong move could crush her dreams...

Can Cindy find the proof she needs, or will this villain punch down her last hope?

Apple Dumpling Murder is the second book in the festive paranormal cozy series, Christmas Catastrophe Mysteries. If you like kind-hearted heroines, furry sidekicks, and a dash of mistletoe magic, then you'll love Trixie Silvertale's seasonal secrets.

Read *Apple Dumpling Murder* to blind bake a killer today!

Features recipes from Cindy's bakery!

USA TODAY BESTSELLING AUTHOR

TRIXIE SILVERTALE

APPLE DUMPLING MURDER

Christmas Catastrophe Mysteries

Silver Shoals

Sittin' On A Goldmine Productions, L.L.C.

pr@sittinonagoldmine.co

www.sittinonagoldmine.co

ISBN: 978-1-952739-23-1

Cover Design © Sittin' On A Goldmine Productions, L.L.C.

Trixie Silvertale
Apple Dumpling Murder: Paranormal Cozy Mystery : a novel / by Trixie Silvertale — 1st ed.
[1. Paranormal Cozy Mystery — Fiction. 2. Cozy Mystery — Fiction. 3. Amateur Sleuths — Fiction. 4. Female Sleuth — Fiction. 5. Wit and Humor — Fiction.] 1. Title.

CHAPTER 1

*T*he chorus of "White Christmas" drifts merrily from the vintage speakers in my cozy bakery. Back when I was living under a dome of magic at the North Pole and training to take over my father's business, the constant barrage of Christmas carols drove me insane.

Today, standing behind my fully stocked pastry case at Yuletide Me Over Bakery, everything feels like it turned out for the best.

I have a steady stream of loyal customers, and the overflow seating area that used to be the next-door yarn shop is nearly bursting at the seams with seasonal tourists. It was definitely the right move to add coffee — in all its forms — to my menu.

Adding an actual barista was also a good move. Despite her initial sullen nature, hiring Jasmine, the former hostess from Sherman's Café across the street, surprisingly worked in my favor. I knew in my heart she was on the Nice List. One of the many merry traits I inherited from Papa, or, as you know him — Santa.

After a brief adjustment period, being surrounded by kindness and the celebration of year-round Christmas lifted Jasmine's spirits. Plus, she's an absolute genius with coffee drinks.

"Ronnie? Ronnie, your order is up." My land-lord and self-appointed crime-solving advisor, Ronnie Schmenkel, and I have formed a special bond. His wife was a legendary baker in Silver Shoals, and sadly passed away the year before I arrived. When he found out I would open a bakery in the space that once housed her precious creations, he passed her well-used personal cookbooks along to me.

What a treasure! The recipes are stellar, and each delicious gem calls for a dollop of love.

Ronnie hobbles toward the counter and balances on his four-pronged cane as a gnarled hand grabs for his steaming mug of black coffee and a piping-hot apple dumpling fresh from the oven — both sharing one large plate so he can carry it himself. Early on, he made sure I knew he didn't expect to be fussed over.

"That there looks good enough to eat, Cindy." Ronnie attempts to press a few bills into my hand, but I wave them away with a gentle flick of my wrist. He chuckles as he shuffles off to find a vacant table.

"Jazz, I'll be in the back working on another batch of scrumptious cinnamon rolls. We already sold out, and there's still the lunch rush to worry about."

Jasmine's relaxed shoulders and subtle grin project the portrait of contentment as her fingers fly over the knobs and levers on the fancy espresso machine she insisted we would need.

Stepping into the homey kitchen fills my heart to overflowing. All these delicious aromas are mine. Sure, I rely on some of Connie's recipes and others from the North Pole elves, but I'm doing all the baking myself. And I love it!

Leaving my protected home at the North Pole, and telling Santa Claus I wasn't ready to take over the business, was one of the hardest things I've ever had to do in my 116 years of life. But it was absolutely the right choice.

Over the past year, I've made several new friends while managing to keep my true identity as Santa's only daughter a secret. I also acquired the additional space across the foyer after the yarn shop closed — because of the death of the owner. And, finally, I've learned how to drive a human car!

Jingle bells! It's the best year yet.

This season always brings a little homesickness, though. There's no place like home during the weeks before Christmas. Everything is running in high gear, and my rosy-cheeked father is at his jolliest. The best way to keep the heartache at bay is to stay busy. That's definitely the half-elf part of me talking. I may not like to make toys or deliver them, but I can get lost in a batch of cinnamon rolls!

Taking one of my favorite recipes from my North Pole baking mentor, whose actual name is Cinnamon Roll, I make the necessary adjustments. I have to replace things like reindeer milk with cow's milk. At first, I missed the familiar flavors of home, but I would practically swear by these modified recipes now. Well, I would *never* swear, but you get the idea.

The enriched dough comes together nicely — springy and elastic — and I place it in the proving drawer to double in size. Meanwhile, I check on Connie Schmenkel's secret marinating raisins to see how they're plumping up. Just as I'm about to begin my cinnamon butter, there's a ruckus in the retail area.

Jasmine pokes her shimmering head of sleek brown waves around the corner. "You better get out here."

"Oh dear. Hope it's not serious." Dusting the flour from my hands, I straighten my smudged green apron and take a deep breath. I emerge from the back just in time to see Ronnie using his cane to steady himself as he climbs from a teetering stool onto a bistro table.

Everyone in the room takes a collective gasp, and I surge forward in case I'm forced to catch this octogenarian high flyer.

He waves me back and clears his throat. "Don't worry about me, little lady." He shakes his metal cane in the air to get everyone's attention. As if he doesn't already have it with this stunt he pulled.

"I have an announcement to make." Ronnie pushes his thinning grey hair out of his eyes.

Stragglers from the overflow room jockey for space near the door. Before they can settle in, those same people are jostling left and right and looking down.

My father's most trusted advisor, Artikoa, bursts through the crowd, takes one look at Ronnie, and sits fidgeting beside me.

This particular advisor happens to be an enchanted arctic fox Papa sent to watch over me. In this human world, he's forced to pretend to be an exotic yet domesticated canine. And, in private, he complains about it endlessly. Since we're in public, I'm spared his usual litany of injustices.

Arti yips once, and Ronnie looks down with warm affection. "Well, if it isn't that feisty pup, Arti! So glad you could join us. You're part of this, too."

Now, Artikoa becomes still and seems genuinely interested.

Satisfied that he has everyone's attention, Ronnie launches into his announcement. "Won't you all join me in a round of applause for Cindy and her amazing treats at Yuletide Me Over Bakery?"

Applause and cheers fill the room as they bounce off the large plate-glass windows and are absorbed by the colorful array of puffy winter coats, pom-pom-topped stocking caps, and wool scarves.

My cheeks turn nearly as cherry-red as my father's as embarrassment washes over me.

"Hear. Hear." Ronnie instigates another round of applause and nearly drops his cane. "I want everyone to hear it here first. I'm changing my will."

There are a few soft gasps, but overall the silence deepens.

"I'm going to leave the bakery and this entire

building to Cindy Claus. She has proven a helpful, contributing member of the Silver Shoals community over this past year, and I can't think of more capable hands to take over when I'm gone."

There's a light smattering of applause, but, in general, many expressions tilt toward sadness.

The concept of death is quite new to me. My father is half angel and, while not immortal, has already lived for several thousand years. And my mother is an elven queen. Another seriously long-lived bloodline. Since my arrival in the human world, I've had to deal with mortality — far more up close and personal than I would have hoped.

My previous upstairs neighbor owned the yarn shop that I recently acquired and remodeled as my overflow seating. She was an interesting woman. One minute she could be your best friend, and the next, well . . . My mother always told me if you don't have something nice to say, it's best to eat a cookie. That doesn't sound exactly right, but you know what I mean.

The kind, bright-eyed local medical examiner, Keith Winters, steps forward to help Ronnie climb down from his precarious perch on my table.

Once my landlord is safely on the floor, I sidle up next to him and slip an arm around his shoulders. "Ronnie, please don't do that. I'm sure you have kids or relatives who would benefit from this building. I appreciate the gesture, but it really isn't necessary."

He waves away my words with a grand swing of his thin arm. "Pshaw. My kids moved away twenty years ago, and I'm lucky if I get a Christmas card from either one of them. The only relatives I have in town are Sven and his brood. He already owns the building where he houses his sign shop, and I can't imagine he needs a job as a landlord with all he's got going on at home."

At the word landlord, another flush reaches my cheeks. My big blue eyes meet Keith's inviting green ones, and he offers a wistful tilt of the head and a shrug of his narrow, athletic shoulders.

"I s'pose you'll be my landlord then, Cindy."

Giggling, I cover my face with one hand and shake my head. "I don't know the first thing about being a landlord. I barely know how to run a bakery."

This draws head shakes from both Ronnie and Keith. Keith is the first to speak. "We all know that's not true. This bakery is about the most amazing thing to happen to Silver Shoals in a long time. Other than *your* arrival, of course."

His perfect mouth curves, and his eyes sparkle with something more than a compliment.

Convinced I'll never win this argument, I pat Ronnie on the shoulder and bow in defeat. "I'm not going to argue with you, but I'm certain you're not going anywhere, anytime soon. You're as strong as a full-grown reindeer."

Ronnie kisses his two fingertips and points them toward heaven. "From your mouth to God's ears, Cindy."

CHAPTER 2

After the chaos of the lunch rush slides into a peaceful lull, I discover we're out of eggs! That's highly unacceptable at a bakery.

"Jasmine, can you watch the store while I run down to the Piggly Wiggly?"

"'Course."

She carries a bin full of dirty dishes into the back room as I grab my red-nosed Rudolph purse and run out the front door. Halfway down the steps, I realize I'm still wearing my flour-covered apron, and run back in to hang it in the kitchen. The neck loop catches on my messy pony, pulling out the hair clip. "Oh, reindeer poop." I have to scrape my wild red hair back into submission before leaving.

As I return to the front door, Artikoa prances down the steps from my upstairs apartment with an irritatingly smug look on his sharp fox face.

It's impossible for me to ignore him. "Jasmine's in the back room. Do you want to accompany me to the Piggly Wiggly?"

He swishes his fluffy snow-white tail and darts out the doggy door beside the entrance without a moment's hesitation.

"I'll take that as a yes." Out on the street, clear of any stragglers in the bakery, Artikoa finally speaks. "Did you have any idea Mr. Schmenkel would be making such an announcement today?"

Scrunching up my face and throwing both mittened hands in the air, I groan. "Me? No. I had no idea."

He pauses his delicate stride and sits on the snow-dusted sidewalk. "Perhaps we should notify your father."

Despite the progress I've made creating a friendship with Santa's former spy, it still raises prickles like icicles when he mentions reporting-in to Papa.

"There's nothing to report, Arti. Ronnie made a silly announcement. Nothing's official, and he said he's changing his will. It could be ages before anything happens to him. I don't know that much about human life spans, but he seems healthy enough."

Artie yips and races off.

When we first came to Silver Shoals, I was quite offended by these sudden mood swings. Now I've learned this behavior means humans are approaching. And me having a conversation with my arctic fox/dog is not something we want anyone to overhear.

"Cindy?"

Spinning on the heel of my winter boot, I have to crane my neck to gaze into the heavily bearded face of Sven Tollesson.

Ignoring the stale odor, I deliver my merriest greeting. "Hello! How's business?"

He exhales slowly. "Funny you should ask. It's not great. The wife and I were kinda counting on Ronnie gifting us that property. The money from the rents would really help us through my off-season, dontcha know?"

Oh dear. Complications. Exactly the kind of thing Artikoa warned me about.

"So Ronnie promised the building to you? This *will* that he talked about changing — right now it says you get the building. Is that right?"

Sven scrapes his knuckles through his blond beard, and a slow-burning anger flashes in his eyes. "Nothing against you, Cindy. I know you didn't instigate this. Just— Well, you runnin' that bakery . . . It reminds him of Connie, God rest her, and he never could think straight where she was concerned."

I have to think fast to defuse this situation and keep Artikoa from contacting Papa. "I don't want to cause any problems for you and your family, Sven. Let me talk to Ronnie. I'm sure I can make him see the error of his ways. After all, I don't know the first thing about owning a property. You and your wife would be much better at it."

The simmering unrest in his tawny-brown eyes cools, and he lowers his chin. "I told Mona you'd see the right side of things." He lumbers off down the sidewalk like a circus bear on two legs as Artikoa races back.

"Anything I should be concerned about?"

Part of me wants to tell him, but a larger part of me knows he'll simply use it as an excuse to contact Santa and sell me out. I'll take a couple days to get everything sorted out, and by the time Papa visits on Christmas Eve, everything will be right as reindeer bells. "Nope. Just having a chat. Let's get down to the Piggly Wiggly and get those eggs. I need to get home and have myself a little nap before I plan tomorrow's baking sessions."

The sly fox runs ahead, lifts his nose high in the air, and seems to grin. "I'm afraid I won't be joining you on the shopping trip, Cynthia. Smells like time to hunt."

With that, he darts down the alley toward the wilderness surrounding the great lake spilling out of Silver Shoals.

After grabbing several dozen eggs, two boxes of candy canes, and five bags of mini marshmallows, I head to the register.

"Hi, Mitch. What's the owner doing running a cash register?"

"My gal Dottie called in sick today. Well, her dog was sick, and that little guy's like a child to her. Have to take the good with the bad where employees are concerned." He scratches his pushbroom of a mustache pleasantly as he rings up my items. "How are things going at your bakery?"

"As efficient as a factory of elves prepping for Christmas." Oh boy! You'd think I'd have learned my lesson by now. Quick subject change. "Did you hear about the announcement Ronnie made?" I may not know everything about the human world, but this last year in my tiny town has taught me that nothing travels faster than gossip, except maybe Santa's sleigh.

Mitch inhales deeply, puffs out his doughy cheeks, and makes a noise that reminds me of an anxious baby seal. "I sure did. I don't have to tell you, Sven isn't gonna take that well."

"Oh, I'll have a little chat with Ronnie. I'm sure I can change his mind. He certainly doesn't need to leave the building to me, and it sure sounds like Sven could use the extra income."

Mitch bags the last of my items and leans forward. "You don't say? Are Sven and the missus having financial trouble?"

Oops! It seems I may have accidentally shared Sven's personal business. Cookie crumbs!

"I better get back to the bakery. Thanks for your help, Mitch."

Loading my groceries into a cart, I push toward home with the determination of a junior reindeer team.

The need to speak to Ronnie sooner rather than later overwhelms me. I park the cart in the little spot in the alleyway behind my bakery and head down to Shallow Shoals.

The local watering hole is the place to find Ronnie at this time of day.

The timeworn brick exterior of this crumbling pillar of our community whispers "out of business," but I know a welcoming atmosphere waits inside.

A quick scan of the dilapidated interior of "The Shallows" reveals two regulars sitting on wobbly stools at the bar, chatting with the owner, Gunnar.

There's no sign of Ronnie.

Waving to Gunnar, I ask, "Have you seen Ronnie this morning?"

A huge grin splits his moon-pie face. "Well, how are you doin' now, Cindy? Ronnie hasn't darkened my door. Which is odd, you know. Usually, he heads here straight after he finishes fillin' his belly at your place." Gunnar pats his own ample gut.

We share a light chuckle. "If he shows up, you tell him I'm looking for him, okay?"

"You betcha, Cindy." Gunnar hoists his thick left thumb in the air and waves it in my direction.

A once confusing gesture, which Keith has since explained to me. Now that I'm familiar with the subtleties, I return the thumbs up and rush back up the street to my bakery.

I wish I had time to borrow Jasmine's car and drive out to Ronnie's place, but I've got to pop those cinnamon rolls in the oven so they'll be fresh for the end-of-day clients grabbing treats on their way home from work.

I hope Mr. Schmenkel wasn't upset when I told him I didn't want the building. Refusing a gift isn't normally in my nature. My papa always told me that a gift is more important to the giver. I learned at a very young age to find something good in any present I received. Papa says the expression of gratitude is what truly fills the giver's heart with joy. If I somehow offended Ronnie, I'd feel terrible.

CHAPTER 3

*J*asmine has finished cleaning the afternoon's mountain of dishes. She carefully stacked mugs, plates, and silverware on the counter behind the register.

The idea of sharing the operation of my bakery with someone else did not appeal to me — initially. Artikoa and his all-knowing amber eyes insisted I would need the help. I certainly won't be telling him he was right.

"Thanks for looking after things. I'll be in the back finishing up those cinnamon rolls if you need anything."

"Always got your back, boss." She pours herself a cup of coffee. "I think we're golden, for now. I'm gonna take a quick break before we get swamped." Jasmine grabs a Santa's Surprise cookie and heads to a table to sit down and rest her feet. "How'd it go with Ronnie?"

The guilt of having possibly offended my first real friend in the human world pinches my features. "I couldn't find him. He wasn't at The Shallows, and I didn't have time to drive out to his house. Would you mind if I borrowed your car later?"

She chews thoughtfully on the peanut butter and chocolate treat and smirks. "On one condition."

"Anything. What do you need?"

"Promise me we'll close on December 24th and 25th."

The idea of not working on Christmas is brand-new to me. It's literally the North Pole's busiest time of year. However, I'm learning that things in the human world are very different from my isolated little bubble in the Arctic. "Of course. I've been telling everyone to pick up their orders by the 23rd, so I can't see any reason to be open on Christmas. You can absolutely have two days off."

Her eyes widen in surprise.

A warming thought pops into my head. "And as your Christmas present, how about I pay you for those two days? Even though you won't have to work — or come in. You can stay home. But I'll pay you anyway." Stumbling over my words at the end, I struggle to make sure she understands what I'm saying and how it's meant to be a gift.

"Wow. That's supes sweet of you. My old boss wouldn't even give us a sick day." Jasmine and I exchange a strained expression. Neither of us wants to discuss Sherman, her former boss, in any detail.

Grabbing my green apron off the hook, I slip it over my head and get to work on those delicious, gooey cinnamon and caramel rolls.

As I pop open the large double doors on the commercial oven, an odd chill grips my shoulders.

Was that a voice? After I close the oven doors, I hear the sound a second time.

Oooooh . . . That definitely sounded like a voice.

Scanning the back room, I note a disturbance in the air above my worktable.

Maybe it's the little angel part of me, but somehow, I know it's the spirit of someone who has crossed over.

"Hi. I think I can see you. How can I help?"

After I acknowledge the disturbance in the air, a figure takes shape from out of the mist.

It appears to be a woman.

She's elderly, for a human, and there's something about her that seems familiar. "Do I know you?" Hmmm. She's not an elf. She's definitely human.

The being swirls toward the open cookbook lying beside my cinnamon roll recipe from the North Pole. Her vaporous hand waves at the cookbook and back toward her ethereal body.

"Connie? Are you Connie Schmenkel?" The apparition seems to glow. But once we've established her identity, her features become a mask of worry. She's gesturing, pointing, and swirling with chaos all at once.

"Connie, is something wrong? Are you in pain?" Her luminous eyes glow with a mix of panic and retribution.

My sparse experience with human lifespans, death, and what must make up their afterlife limits the help I can offer.

The spirit points once again to the cookbook. And then to me.

"No. It's not my cookbook. If you're Connie Schmenkel, that's your old cookbook. It was given to me."

Her shimmering hand seems to become more solid, and she points at me rapidly.

"Me? I'm Cindy."

She shakes her vaporous head, and once again points to the cookbook and then to me.

"Yes. The cookbook was given to me . . . Given to me! By your husband, Ronnie."

She swirls toward me, and an icy flash raises chill bumps all over my arms.

"Is something wrong with Ronnie?"

Before Connie can answer, Jasmine walks into the back. "Are you talking to someone?"

Connie's ghost vanishes, along with any chance I had of getting additional information.

"Jazz, I don't know why, but I think something might really be wrong with Ronnie. When the timer goes off, pull these out and tip them upside down on the cooling racks." Leaving my creation in the oven gives me a moment of panic, but I can't ignore Connie's urgent message from beyond.

"No prob."

"Also, I'm sorry, but I'm going to need to borrow your car right now. I'll try to get back for the late afternoon rush. But— I'm sorry. I can't explain."

Jasmine runs to her purse behind the counter and retrieves her keys. "Here. It's parked right on the street in front of that vegetarian place that re-placed the café."

I'd love to sit around and chat about the delicious vegetarian restaurant that seemed to appear magically across the street when Sherman's Café went out of business, but I simply grab the keys and rush out the front door.

Blizzards! I'm still wearing my apron, but there's no time to worry about that.

As I drive toward Ronnie's home on the outskirts of our quaint town, a sick feeling tumbles around my insides.

Somewhere in the back of my head I can hear Artikoa yipping on about speed limits and other rules of the road, but all I can think is that the faster I get to Mr. Schmenkel's house, the sooner I'll know he's okay. Thank the angels that I learned how to drive.

His truck is in the driveway. That's a good sign.

Parking behind his vehicle, I hurry through the knee-deep snow to his front door.

Maybe he has someone in the neighborhood who shovels his walk for him, but it hasn't snowed in over two weeks. Maybe he uses a side door.

A soft knock on the front door produces no result. Knocking more firmly doesn't do any better.

Peering through the double panes of glass in the front door as I ring the doorbell, the uneasy feeling in my stomach grows.

Ronnie still doesn't answer.

I open the storm door and try the handle on the thick wooden door. It's not locked.

Most humans would probably feel misgivings about entering a home uninvited. Being raised by Santa Claus, I have no such instinct. These people have an entire holiday dedicated to my papa sneaking into their houses and leaving gifts. My inner "Claus" takes over. I twist the cold metal handle, wishing I'd grabbed my mittens, and step inside.

As I enter Ronnie's house, the tops of my ears tingle.

Something is wrong.

Mama always told me if I'd been born with elven ears, I wouldn't get that sensation. She claimed it's like a phantom limb. Since my time in the human world, I've begun to notice the tingle is a warning to be on high alert.

There's a kettle whistling angrily on his stove, and a stale, coppery smell hanging heavy in the air.

Rushing to the kitchen, I turn the burner off. "Ronnie? Ronnie, it's Cindy."

It suddenly occurs to me that Mr. Schmenkel might be in the restroom.

"Ronnie, are you indisposed?"

Still no response.

As I round the corner from the small dining room into the shamrock-green forward living room, I see winter boots with the toes pointing down.

My stomach feels as though it's seeking refuge in my throat.

One step further . . .

There's a body attached to those boots.

Without thinking, I rush forward and roll him over. "Ronnie?"

Silence. Deathly quiet.

Tears well up in my eyes when I realize I'm far too late to save my dear friend.

Leaning back against his unapologetically plaid sofa, tears stream down my cheeks. If only I'd figured out who Connie was — what she wanted — if I had gotten here sooner . . .

Stumbling back to Ronnie's kitchen, I lift his pale-yellow phone from the cradle and dial the all-too-familiar 9-1-1.

"Hi, yes, I need an ambulance or something."

The operator asks the nature of my emergency, and I can barely get an explanation out between the tears.

She asks my name.

"Cindy. Cindy Claus."

The woman takes a deep breath and mumbles something I can't quite make out. She instructs me to stay on the line as she dispatches deputies and an ambulance.

It doesn't take long for the sirens to draw near.

"They're here. Should I hang up now?"

The operator instructs me to hang up, let the deputies in, and share my story with them.

The first thing that pops into my head is how terribly this all went the last time I tried that.

Deputy Saul Rivera is the first through the door. "Miss Claus? What's going on?"

Defensiveness creeps into my voice despite my best efforts. "I came to talk to Ronnie. He didn't answer. The door was unlocked." Intermittent sobs interrupt my report. Pressing one hand to my mouth, I gesture with the other. "He's in the living room."

Saul brushes past me as another vehicle rolls into the driveway. Keith Winters hops out, takes one look at me, and tilts his stocking-cap-covered head in concern as he approaches.

"Cindy, what happened?"

"It's Ronnie. I think he's dead."

Keith exhales and shakes his head. He always said kind things about Ronnie, and the death clearly upsets him.

"Why don't you wait in your car, Cindy? I'll come out after I finish collecting evidence."

"Evidence?"

"Yup. Dispatch said you mentioned there was a head wound. Right?"

The image flashes to mind, and I shudder. "I thought maybe he hit his head when he fell."

Keith places a calming hand on my shoulder. "That's entirely possible. I won't know until I look at the scene. Please go wait in your car."

Sitting in Jasmine's car, time seems to stand still. When it happens for my father, it's wonderful and magical and everyone gets their presents on time. When it happens to me, someone's dead. Sure is a good thing I'm not the one sailing around the world in one night!

After what seems like an eternity, the paramedics wheel out Ronnie's body. It's not hooked up to any equipment. It's completely covered under a sheet as they solemnly load him into their vehicle. Mr. Winters exchanges words with them and Deputy Rivera before heading to my car.

Keith stops, opens the door, and shakes his head. "I was really hoping we weren't too late. There's nothing I like more than finding a pulse on a body. Unfortunately, my initial investigation puts Ronnie's time of death between 10:00 a.m. and noon."

A heartbroken shudder shakes my shoulders. "I never got to talk to him. If I'd known this morning —" My voice catches in my throat, and a fresh wave of tears trickle down my cheeks.

He casts his eyes to the side and sighs. "Deputy

Rivera is going to need a statement from you. Don't let him rattle you. You had nothing to do with this."

"What? I would never hurt Ronnie. How can he even think that?"

Before Keith can offer any words of wisdom, Deputy Rivera approaches and waves him off. The deputy's deep-brown eyes lock onto me, and my heart thumps in my chest as he leans closer. "Miss Claus, do you want to give me your statement here, or will you come down to the station?"

"I'll give it here, if it's all the same to you." I have no intention of going anywhere near that sheriff's station.

"Where were you between 10:00 a.m. this morning and noon?"

"Let's see . . . I was at the bakery — Oh, then I went to the Piggly Wiggly to pick up eggs and a few other items. Why?"

Rivera ignores my question and clenches his square jaw. "I'm told you and the victim had a disagreement this morning. What was that about?"

"Disagreement? No. No. Ronnie announced he was going to give me the bakery — the entire building. Afterward, I told him I didn't want it. That he didn't have to do that."

"Were you upset?" He squares his shoulders and taps his pen.

"No. I was flattered that he wanted to, but I told him he should give it to family."

Deputy Rivera lifts his chin, revealing a few hairs he missed in this morning's shaving. "And why did you follow him back to his house?"

My eyes must be as wide as reindeer hooves. "Follow him? No. I didn't follow him. I went to the Piggly Wiggly. Then back to the bakery. Then I—" Oops. I can't really tell him about seeing Connie's ghost. "When I finished the cinnamon rolls, I asked Jasmine if I could borrow her car. I only arrived a few minutes before I called 9-1-1."

He scratches some notes on his pad. "We'll confirm your alibi."

"Alibi? It's not an alibi. It's the truth."

"I'll decide what the truth is after I've verified this information. You're free to go, but don't leave town." The bleak winter sun shoots a glint of gold off his badge as he turns.

"I wouldn't." What makes him think I'm going to leave town? Where would I go? The only people I know are in Silver Shoals. Well, people. I can't possibly run back to the North Pole with this mess hanging over my head. Papa would never let me leave again.

Deputy Rivera slams my car door shut and returns to his vehicle.

Sounds like Ronnie's death was no accident. I

don't like the idea of someone taking my friend's life and getting away with it. Arti and I learned quite a lot about investigating from retired deputy Mr. Schmenkel. I never thought I'd have to use those skills to solve his murder, but I won't hesitate to do it.

CHAPTER 4

*T*he final hours at the bakery wear on, and I can't shake the hollow feeling in my heart. This is the first true friend I've ever lost to death, and it all feels like a bad dream. If only I could wake up and see Ronnie's curmudgeonly face shuffling toward the counter to order his favorite apple dumpling with extra whipped cream. But I'll never get to see that again. I'll never get to trade jokes, refill his coffee, or wave away his cash when he tries to pay.

There are so many things I've taken for granted. Living among humans and their mortality brings life into sharper focus.

I won't have centuries of moments with all the good people of Silver Shoals. Maybe I'll have months or, hopefully, years. But that's all. I need to make more of an effort to make each moment count. Squeeze the best out of each memory . . . to truly live.

"Hey there, I'm headed home."

The voice of my employee shatters my melancholy. "Oh, of course. Thanks again for letting me borrow your car. I'll see you tomorrow."

Jasmine tosses her red apron into the hamper and offers a casual wave as she exits the bakery.

As is my habit, I follow her to the front door and lock it after she leaves.

Artikoa hasn't returned from his hunt, and I desperately need someone to talk to. Dusting my hands on my apron, I climb the short flight of stairs to the landing, take the familiar right turn, and climb the second flight of stairs. Finding myself outside Keith's door, I give a light knock.

No answer.

No surprise. I'm sure he's still at the station, or wherever he conducts his medical investigations.

At first, it was odd to have someone living in the apartment where Betty Troup died, but Keith had a great explanation. He said that he deals with death every day, and he believes the good guys win more than they lose. As a medical examiner, he wouldn't mind cleaning the place up, and then he could finally get out from under Deputy Rivera's roof. He was grateful for the room he rented there, but he'd do just about anything to have his own place.

When he put it like that, it made sense. I wish he were home right now.

My shoulders slump as I slip the key into my lock and stumble into my dark apartment. I haven't eaten since breakfast, but I have no appetite.

I'm still wearing my apron — again. I drop it on the floor and crawl into bed, fully dressed.

I should probably set some kind of alarm to make sure I don't sleep through my evening planning session, but all that seems so unimportant.

A gentle tapping on my door pulls me from dreamless slumber.

Sitting up in bed, I rub the last mists of sleep from my eyes. Moonlight peaks through my window and casts a silvery glow over my holiday decorations. I must've slept for some time. Where are my manners? "Who is it?"

"It's Keith. I thought maybe you'd like to talk. Mind if I come in?"

"Sure, let me—" There's not much point in unlocking the door. I never locked it behind myself. Good thing Arti isn't here to chew me out. "Sure, come on in."

Keith steps into my shadowy apartment and stops. "May I turn on a light?"

The only thing running through my mind is how messed up I must look. I've never been a self-conscious person, but every time I'm around Keith, I seem to worry about my hair or what I'm wearing. Strange. "Go ahead. I must warn you, I was sleeping."

"Oh, gosh. I'm sorry to wake you, Cindy. Should I come back in the morning?"

"No. No. Now is fine. In the morning, I'll be up to my elbows in dough at the bakery. Come on in and I'll make us some peppermint hot chocolate. Artikoa isn't here." Melting snowballs! I'm alone with Mr. Winters! Now I feel self-conscious again.

Keith flicks on the light and takes a seat in one of my plush green-velvet armchairs. He turns the chair to face the kitchen, and his eyes twinkle with amusement as I stumble around collecting ingredients for the cocoa.

"You look great, by the way."

I tuck my fiery red hair behind my ears and shrug. "Thanks."

"Glad to hear you were able to get a little sleep. It can be quite traumatizing to discover something like you stumbled on this afternoon. Since my job puts that sort of thing in front of me on a regular basis, I've developed a thick skin, as they say. Did you want to talk about it?"

Images from this afternoon's horrible discovery flash through my mind, and my stomach clenches in protest. "No. I don't even want to think about it. I just want to pretend it was a bad dream. One I'll wake up from, and—" Tears gather in the corners of my eyes, and I grab a dish towel to wipe them away.

Keith is on his feet in a flash and walks toward the kitchen. "I'm so sorry this happened, Cindy. But it's not a bad dream. It's a bad reality. Ronnie's not coming back, and he only has us to make sure the person who did this pays for their crime. You were a ton of help on the Betty Troup case. Can I count on you to share any information you might find if you look into Ronnie's death?"

"I'm not sure how I can help with medical examinations." My chest tightens.

"Oh, I forgot to tell you. Rivera was so impressed with my work on the Betty Troup case, he's finally letting me do the job I was hired for — medical investigator."

Searching my drawer for a wooden spoon, I answer absently, "That's different?"

"Oh yeah. In these small towns, we need all the boots on the ground we can get. Now, I'll be able to leave the lab and officially investigate crime scenes. I'll still have all my other duties — but — you know."

I didn't, but maybe it would make more sense tomorrow. "Sure. If you say so."

"So, will you help me out?" His tone holds equal measures of pleading and admiration.

As the chocolate melts and swirls into the milk, the thin ribbons draw my attention for a moment, and the pain slips from the forefront. "Yeah. You can count on me."

Keith steps closer, and I feel that familiar heat flush my cheeks. Stirring faster to distract myself sends a bit of hot chocolate sloshing over the side of the pan.

He reaches out, turns off the burner, takes the spoon from my hand, and places it in the spoon rest. "Cindy, I want you to know I'm saying this as a friend. You look like you could use a hug."

The storm of emotions gathering at the corner of my eyes bursts forth, and I throw my arms around his neck.

Keith hugs almost as good as my papa, and he smells like cinnamon with a hint of antiseptic. He holds me until the sobbing subsides, then he hands me the dishtowel. "I don't know if you have tissues."

Shaking my head, I take the towel. "I'm not

used to crying this much. I suppose I'll have to invest in a box or two if this keeps up."

"Everyone gets to deal with death in their own way." He steps around me to pour the hot cocoa into two mugs, places a candy cane in each, and offers me a wink. "Shall we have a seat?"

Keith adjusts the chairs so that they are facing each other with the small round coffee table between. We place our steaming mugs on the dark mahogany table and settle into the chairs. The moonlight reflecting off the snowy hills outside my window adds a lovely glow to the room.

"I know you probably don't want to talk about it, Cindy, but can you tell me exactly what happened when you got to Ronnie's house?" Keith wraps his hands around his mug, and for the first time, I notice how carefully trimmed he keeps his fingernails.

"Do you get manicures? That's what it's called, right?" Even after a year in the human world, there are still terms I'm struggling with.

"Yup. The deputies love to give me a hard time about that. As a medical investigator, I spend most of my days tugging latex gloves on and off. If I have any amount of length in my fingernails or a rough corner here or there, all bets are off. Plus, manicures are pretty relaxing. I can take you some time."

Is that a date? Jasmine is always going on dates. The way she's explained them, it seems far more complicated. But he did offer to take me somewhere. Oh dear! Uncharted icebergs! "Take me? Is it somewhere local?"

He shakes his head. "No. Believe it or not, the best place is over in Timber Town. They have a slightly larger population, and a few strip malls have survived the recent economic chaos. Let me know if you ever take a day off. I'm happy to make an appointment for two."

That definitely sounds like a date. I'll check with Jasmine tomorrow, to be sure. "Actually, I promised Jasmine we would close the bakery on the 24th and 25th. So, I'll have those days off."

Keith chokes on his peppermint hot chocolate as he chuckles. He pats his chest and struggles to clear his throat. "Pretty much everyone will have those days off, Cindy. We'll figure something out." Stirring his cocoa with the candy cane, it slowly sinks into the chocolaty liquid — vanishing from sight. "Now, tell me about Ronnie's."

I relay the day's events as best I can. But each time images swirl to the forefront, I push them away.

"That's good information. Did you see anything lying on the ground near Ronnie's — near Ronnie?"

Drawing a ragged breath, I force myself to examine the unsavory mental picture. "Was there a rolling pin?"

Keith exhales and places his mug on the small table. "Yup. That's the thing that has Deputy Rivera looking at you as a prime suspect."

"What? I didn't take a rolling pin to Ronnie's. I drove Jasmine's car out there to talk to him and I didn't have anything with me. Plus, that was marble. Definitely not my rolling pin. I stick with good old-fashioned larch. My papa's favorite."

He bobs his head thoughtfully and chews the inside of his left cheek. "I've said it before, and I'll say it again, I believe you. I'm certain you didn't have anything to do with what happened to Ronnie. We need to find out where that rolling pin came from."

Silence falls between us as I drift into thought.

I've been to Ronnie's house before, and Papa always told me I have an excellent memory. That was part of the reason I was able to create such an amazing route for him and his sleigh. I'd ridden with him several times as a child, and I remembered the various obstacles that slowed us down.

Letting my mind drift back to previous visits to Ronnie's house, ones where I didn't discover a corpse, I can picture standing in the kitchen waiting for him to boil water for his coffee and my instant hot chocolate. He refused to make a more complicated version from scratch. As I scan through the memory, I see a small plaque on the wall with a narrow bookshelf— "It was Connie's! He had a little memorial in the corner of the kitchen. There was a photo of her with her favorite recipe for strawberry rhubarb pie. It was framed above the shelf. And on the shelf was her marble-and-maple rolling pin. Ronnie said he thought about giving it to me, but he couldn't part with it. That was Connie's rolling pin. You have to tell Deputy Rivera."

A genuine smile lifts the corners of Keith's mouth as his eyes shine. "I knew you could do it. You're one of a kind, Cindy."

Ignoring the compliment, I march ahead. "Are you going to call Deputy Rivera?" I know Keith has a portable phone. I've seen him use it before.

He glances at the watch on his left wrist. "It's after midnight, Cindy. I'll let him know first thing in the morning."

Worry grips my shoulders and sends an unwelcome chill across my skin. "After midnight? Where's Artikoa?"

Keith hops up from his chair, takes our empty mugs to the sink, and returns to offer me a hand.

He pulls me to my feet and places a comforting arm around my shoulders. "Should we go look for him?"

"For whom?" Keith's nearness has erased whatever thoughts had been bouncing in my brain. I want to lean in and inhale another whiff of that squeaky-clean cinnamon. As I tilt my head in his direction, the doggy door to my apartment blasts open, and a wild-eyed fox lands aggressively on all fours with teeth bared.

"Easy, boy. It's me. Your buddy, Keith."

Arti lifts his nose in the air and sniffs twice. His judgmental eyes fix me with a stare that clearly says we'll be discussing this later.

"Don't worry, Arti. Keith was just leaving. You missed quite a day. Quite an awful day."

Keith gives my shoulders one more squeeze before exiting the apartment.

As soon as I hear his door close across the hall, I collapse onto the chair and tears race down my cheeks as I share the day's tragedy with Artikoa.

CHAPTER 5

I'm not normally a coffee drinker, but by morning the exhaustion of loss has crept into my bones. I brew myself a terrible cup of coffee and hope that it gives me the necessary jolt to make it through this morning's baking.

A couple of regulars have already queued up outside the front door when I make it to the bottom of the steps. I'm still wearing yesterday's snowflake leggings and light-blue sweater, picturing a snowman in a top hat. Fortunately, no one seems to notice.

I unlock the front door and welcome my loyal patrons. Jasmine must have entered through the alleyway, since the doors to the retail area are still locked. I have to give the key a special jiggle to unlock the bakery. Swirls of emotions well up as I recall Ronnie teaching me that trick.

The early risers head straight to the counter, and I slip into the back room with a low wave to Jasmine.

After donning a fresh green apron from the closet, I fall into my usual routine. Quick check of the stock, place a large bowl of eggs on the counter, and remove ten pounds of butter to soften. I get several pots bubbling on the stove; one will become thick raspberry preserves, one is headed toward date filling for my pinwheels, and one holds some melting butter to brush over the dough for today's fresh caramel cinnamon rolls.

As I lose myself in the baking, the hum of Christmas carols fills the room. "White Christmas" seems to top the charts once again. Maybe it's playing on the speakers up front and seeping into my subconscious. Or maybe it's a childish dream of huge white flakes falling on Christmas Day and making my father's visit even more special.

I didn't write him a letter this year. The hand-carved wooden sign he and the elves created to hang outside my bakery last year still makes my heart swell with love every day. I'm sure he'll know what to bring me. After all, he *is* Santa Claus.

Jasmine peeks around the corner. "There's a cop here to see you. Should I send him back?"

"Sure." A quick adjustment to the messy bun I tossed my hair into this morning does little to improve my sleep-deprived appearance. Disappointingly, the cop is not Keith.

Deputy Rivera lifts his square jaw and drags a hand through his dark buzz cut, speckled with an occasional grey hair. His uniform appears freshly pressed, and his badge and nameplate shine as though lit from within. "I have a few more questions for you, Miss Claus."

"No problem. I have to keep an eye on these things on the stove, but ask me anything."

He clears his throat, removes a small notepad from his pocket, and clicks the top of his pen. "We got some new information this morning about the murder weapon. It appears to have been a weapon of opportunity. Can you tell me again why you were at Ron Schmenkel's home?"

The only other creature who can get under my skin this quickly is Artikoa. Even though he's upstairs sound asleep in the apartment, the sensation is all too familiar. "Yes. Ronnie had made an announcement here at the bakery about leaving me this place — the whole building — in his will. I didn't want him to do that, and that was even before I knew how upset Sven was about the change."

Rivera's beady eyes dart up from his notepad. "What's that you said about Tollesson?"

Melting snowballs! "Upset isn't the right word. It was only a conversation. Sven wanted me to know that he and his wife were supposed to inherit this building. That's all."

"Interesting. And you're certain you only went out to the Schmenkel residence for conversation?"

"Of course. Ronnie and I were friends. He was very kind to me. I would never want any harm to come to him. And, like I said, I didn't want him to give me the building. Why would I hurt him?"

"Noted." Deputy Rivera closes his notepad and shoves it in his pocket. "I'm not removing you from the suspect list just yet, but I do have several other people to interview."

"Okay. Would you like a cinnamon roll to go?"

Despite his prickly exterior, my inner Claus knows that he's definitely on the Nice List. He attempts to remain detached, but the mention of a free pastry turns up one corner of Rivera's stern mouth.

"Sure. If it's not too much trouble."

"No trouble at all." I grab a small green pastry box and wedge two gooey cinnamon rolls inside.

"Here ya go. Please let me know if there's anything else I can do."

The hard edge framing his face softens for a moment as he takes the treats. "Thanks, Miss Claus."

The rest of my morning whizzes by faster than elves wrapping presents. When Jasmine sticks her head around the corner, I feel as though I'm returning from some long, inexplicable journey.

"Cindy, do you want to take the first lunch, or should I?"

The sudden realization that I haven't eaten anything since yesterday's breakfast hits me like an iced-over snowball. "I'll go right now if that's okay?"

Jasmine gives me a playful finger gun. "Totes."

Hanging my apron on the hook, I pull the hair tie from my hair and scrape my fingers through the unruly red locks in an attempt to create a presentable ponytail.

I dash across the street, checking both ways for cars, and step into D'lish. This new vegetarian restaurant is the highlight of my dining adventures in Silver Shoals.

"Welcome, Cindy! The usual?" Zahara's golden eyes sparkle with delight. She loves what she does, almost as much as I do.

"Thanks. I think I'll sit down and take a look at

the menu today, Zahara. Do you have any specials?"

She grabs a menu — printed on recycled paper — and takes me to a quaint table by the front window. "I've told you a million times, just call me Z. Everyone else does. And today's special is roasted root vegetables with a side salad of kale, dried cranberries, candied walnuts, and crumbled feta."

"Ooooh! I'll definitely have that — Z." Look at me, getting the hang of human nicknames.

"Excellent choice. Anything to drink?"

"I'd like to try your jasmine tea."

"My pleasure." Z bobs her head, and her tight black curls seem to float in the air momentarily as she spins and heads into the kitchen.

D'lish has an impressive list of teas. Prior to leaving the North Pole, I only drank medicinal preparations at my mother's insistence. Drinking herbal teas for fun is a brand-new and, I have to say, somewhat enchanting experience.

I'm so lucky that this restaurant opened across the street from me. I grew up on a vegetarian diet. In this region full of hunters and anglers, I was finding it hard to locate restaurants that served interesting, veg-friendly dishes. I'll have the occasional fish, one of my father's favorites, but I honestly prefer my mother's way of eating.

With the opening of this lovely place and its extensive menu, I eat lunch here practically every day.

The green-and-white paper currency my mother sent along with me to help me get started has run out. Though, I'm happy to report my bakery has been a profitable endeavor. Artikoa's words, not mine.

Ronnie helps me . . . Ronnie helped me. I guess I have to refer to him in the past tense now. He helped me set up budgets and make charts for sales projections. I'm getting used to visiting the bank to make my weekly deposit and top off my savings account. I'm taking control of my future.

Delicious aromas explode from the kitchen when Z opens the door and returns. The steam rising from the mound of potatoes, turnips, parsnips, carrots, and beets is enough to make me faint in anticipation.

"Oooh! Thank you."

Her full lips spread into a massive grin and she winks.

Spending most of this past year observing the behavior of the humans around me, by mimicry, I learned how to fit in. However, I love eating my meal when it's as warm as possible, so I forgo the human tradition of eating salad first. I dig into my luscious, buttery root vegetables and, when I feel almost full, I switch to the salad — which packs a flavorful punch.

The D'lish décor is such a change from the previous restaurant. Now I dine on bamboo chairs with green-and-gold leaf-patterned cushions that complement the earth-tone walls — plus, I'm surrounded by lush green plants. A treat for an arctic gal. We had tons of plants in the greenhouses, but decorative plants, with no nutritional purpose, are a lovely new experience.

Z returns with my bill and points at my nearly empty plate. "Were you pleased with your lunch, Cindy?"

Wiping the corners of my mouth with the hemp-fabric napkin, I sigh with satisfaction and reply, "You've never let me down, Z."

She glances at the edge of my plate and points. "That looks like dried tomato sauce. Did you put ketchup on your plate?"

"No. Must've been there."

Z rolls her large, expressive eyes and exhales loudly. "Wow. This new guy I hired to wash dishes cuts way too many corners. I'm gonna have to have a talk with him."

"Well, go easy on him. Jasmine was a bit of a problem when she first started, but I tried to catch her doing things right and praise her rather than criticize her for making mistakes."

Zahara tilts her head and nods knowingly. "That's why everyone loves you, Cindy. Your heart is pure gold."

Counting out some bills from my tiny reindeer purse, I ponder those words as I wander back across the street. Heart of pure gold? That seems impossible. Gold is rather heavy and wouldn't actually pump blood. Unless it was some kind of mechanized heart—

SCREEECH!

Icicles! I forgot to look both ways.

Lucky for me, the face staring at me through the windshield belongs to Keith Winters, and he appears more relieved than angry.

As I hurry out of his way, he rolls down his window. "You need to be more careful, Cindy. You're always dreaming up some amazing baked treat, but if you can't safely walk across the street, we'll never get to enjoy it. Keep your head on a swivel, eh?"

"Okay. Thanks for not running me over."

"Any time." He chuckles. "By the way, we found your prints on the rolling pin."

My heart drops into my stomach. "But I—"

Keith waves away my objection. "Don't worry. The rest of the pin was wiped clean. I convinced Deputy Rivera you were set up."

"Set up? How?" My mind races back to the unwelcome image of finding Ronnie. Did I touch the rolling pin when I rolled him over? I can't remember.

"It's not that difficult to plant fingerprints. I'm not saying it's easy, but with a few clean prints to work from and some basic equipment, prints can be duplicated and falsely placed at a crime scene."

"Gosh." I'm struggling to swallow.

"Don't worry. I have other folks to talk to. In fact, I'm on my way to talk to Sven and collect DNA."

"Sven? He wouldn't hurt Ronnie. They're family." My heart thuds, and I feel my stomach lurching dangerously. "Can I come with you?"

"Sorry. No civilians on official interviews." Keith winks. "I'll stop by the bakery for an *unofficial* cup of coffee on my way back to the station."

CHAPTER 6

Standing on the step outside my bakery, my shoulders lose their fight against gravity as I watch Keith's unremarkable grey car disappear down Main Street toward Sven's sign shop. I wonder if he'll find him there? Ronnie's death must've upset Sven. Maybe he went home to be with his family.

The clock above the door in my back room seems to stare down at my afternoon's efforts with disinterest. In fact, it seems more like a painting of a clock than an actual timepiece. Maybe it's broken? I'm certain it's said the same time the last ten times I've checked.

Stepping around the corner, I call out, "Jazz, what time is it?"

"Are you taking another break?"

"No. I was— Not important. I've got to chop up the dried fruit for the apple dumpling filling and . . . Never mind."

Hurrying into the back, I grab a large bowl of prunes, dump them onto my two-foot-by-two-foot butcher's block cutting board, and take out my frustration with a rougher-than-necessary rough chop.

After completing the rest of my prep checklist, I grab a bag of mini chocolate Santas and tear it open, fully intending to fill my belly and remove all evidence that these twenty-one miniature Clauses ever existed.

Before I can get the foil wrapper peeled from even one of my delicacies, Mr. Winters makes his long-awaited appearance.

"Hiya, Cindy. Got a minute to join me for a cup of coffee?" His tone is casual, but he doesn't exactly make eye contact.

I keep my response as level as possible. Of course, it's hard to wipe the guilt from my face as I shove the tiny St. Nicholas menagerie under the worktable.

"Well, sure. Let me finish up, and if you make that coffee a peppermint hot chocolate, I'll join you in the overflow seating area in about five minutes." There's absolutely no reason I can't join him right now, but I'm trying to keep in line with his casual energy.

Keith bites the inside of his cheek as though battling his own thoughts. "If you can make it faster, I'd appreciate it. I don't have much time before I'm expected back at the station."

"Oh. I didn't realize you were in a hurry. I can take a break right now."

His kind and patient tone, as he relays our order to Jasmine, reminds me why I always feel comfortable around him.

When I slip behind the counter to add extra marshmallows to my cocoa, Jasmine elbows me and flashes a wicked grin. "That Keith Winters sure has been drinking a lot of coffee lately." She arches an eyebrow and snickers. As usual, the cheeks I inherited from my papa flush all too easily with a rosy glow.

Taking Keith's coffee from her tray, I carry the two mugs across the foyer and into the adjacent area. When I remodeled the old yarn shop, I attempted to keep the same feel as the bakery's main retail space. Lots of Christmas lights, tons of vintage ornaments, and a consistent red-and-green theme. I even found a vendor who supplies me with Christmas-tree-shaped napkins. I love them.

Keith sits at a table in the back corner. As I approach, the look on his face gives me pause.

"What happened? You can't possibly think Sven is guilty, can you?"

He accepts the coffee and motions for me to take a seat.

"I shouldn't be discussing an ongoing investigation, Cindy." He drops his head for a moment and exhales as he looks up. "Ronnie trusted you, and I hope I can trust you too. The last time anyone can vouch for his whereabouts, Sven was getting incredibly intoxicated at Shallow Shoals. He had a shouting match with Ronnie in the bar, and left shortly after Mr. Schmenkel stomped out in a huff. Doesn't look good."

It strikes me as odd that Gunnar didn't mention this to me. Maybe he knew I was snooping for Keith. "What did Sven have to say for himself?"

"Not much. The sign shop was locked up tight, so I had to drive about fifteen miles out of town to his homestead. His wife was reluctant to let me in, but I'm glad she did. Sven was in no condition to argue with me when I asked if I could take a DNA sample and fingerprints." Keith shrugs. "The consent wouldn't hold up to scrutiny in court, but it will give the deputies something to work with."

I shake my head in disbelief and stir my cocoa as Keith continues.

"Between you and me, I think he was lucky to make it home without getting into a serious vehicular accident. But people do strange things when they're intoxicated. I've been on the job long enough to know that. We can't rule him out. But I'm going to keep following the evidence and see what else we can turn up."

This information about Sven hurts my heart. He seems like a big teddy bear, and he has so many children depending on him. "Was he able to answer any questions? What did he say about the rolling pin?"

"He confirmed he'd seen the rolling pin." Keith takes a sip of coffee and continues, "That it never left the shelf in the kitchen. I've been able to verify it's the murder weapon. Blunt force trauma and a severe brain bleed are what did Ronnie in. Even if you'd found him sooner, there's very little chance he would've survived. So don't beat yourself up about that."

The thought of beating myself up never occurred to me. Must be one of those figures of speech Artikoa loves to mention.

"What happens now?" My hand absently continues to stir my hot chocolate with the shrinking peppermint candy cane.

He exhales heavily and tosses his head slowly from side to side. "I go back to the beginning. I'll head out to Ronnie's house, see if there was something I missed . . . reexamine the body. No one's pushing for a quick funeral, so at least I have time on my side."

Funeral. I've never been to a funeral, but I can't possibly tell Keith. Maybe there's a better way to get the information I need. "With his wife gone, who will plan the service?"

"With what I know of local gossip, that would fall on the doorstep of Sven and Mona. Although, while he's still a suspect, I doubt Deputy Rivera will let him anywhere near the cor— Ronnie."

A sip of hot chocolate triggers an idea. "Ronnie mentioned his will when he was in my bakery. Doesn't the will usually have information about that sort of thing?"

About to take a sip of his coffee, Keith lowers the cup and narrows his gaze. "Ronnie really knew what he was doing when he said you had a knack for this sleuthing thing. That's an excellent point. I'll reach out to their family attorney and see if we can get a copy of the will for the investigation."

A ready smile brightens my face, before I realize it might be considered inappropriate to look happy about memorial services.

Forcing my features to return to somber, I continue, "If there's anything I can do — to help plan the service or prepare food. I'm happy to help. Well, not happy—" My hand goes to my forehead, and, as I shake my head in dismay, several strands of wild red hair release themselves from my half-hearted ponytail.

Keith sets down his cup, reaches across the table, and pats my hand. "I know what you meant, Cindy. I'll get a copy of that will, and if there's anything that you can handle, I'll let you know. In the meantime, this conversation stays between us. Okey dokey?"

My expression leaps from somber to innocent offense. "Of course. I would never tell a secret. I was the best secret keeper at the North Pole." My hand flies up to cover my mouth, and there's absolutely nothing I can do but force myself to laugh. The sound is hollow and insincere.

The great news is, Keith is so preoccupied with this case that he takes my comment at face value and joins my laughter at what he's certain is a joke.

Maybe my brilliant mama knows some type of magic to prevent me from making these incessant verbal blunders.

CHAPTER 7

Sven may have been upset about the possible change in Ronnie's will, but no part of me believes he would hurt his cousin. From everything I've seen, despite the age gap, they were closer than brothers.

I don't think it would be considered interfering with the case if I go and chat with a friend. Besides, I do actually need Sven to paint a matching Yuletide bakery sign on the window of my new seating area.

Artikoa has been moping. He's probably eager to head into the wilderness again. However, his sense of duty has kept him close to my side ever since news of Ronnie's murder spread through the town.

Heading up to the apartment, I unlock the door, glance over my shoulder to make sure no one's within earshot, and invite him to join me.

"It would be helpful. Honest. You might be able to smell something on Sven that will help me figure out this mess. Every little piece of information helps. And you were so much help untangling the whole Betty debacle."

The sly white fox laughs. Not a sound I often hear.

"What's funny?"

"I found a humorous connection between your use of the word untangle and the fact that Miss Troup once owned a yarn shop."

Shrugging, I gesture for him to lead the way out of the apartment. "After you, Mr. Chuckles."

He sulks onto the landing between my door and Keith's, and I secure the door as I've been taught.

"Wait for me outside. I need to grab a treat for Sven."

Arti pushes through the small access door, built for him, and sits on the sidewalk.

I grab a surprise for the sign maker and join the fox.

An icy wind knifes across the great lake and tosses the loose strands of my copper hair every which way.

Arti lifts his nose and inhales deeply. "What a lovely day."

I may be a North Pole girl, but even I have my limits. "I would hardly call it nice, Arti. This wind is brutal. Some days, I definitely miss the protection of Mama's magic bubble."

He shakes his shoulders and fluffs out his spotless white fur. "Nonsense. This is the kind of day I dream of. If everything seems copacetic with Mr. Tollesson, I may take the long way home."

Tightening my treasured gift from Cinnamon Roll, a hand-knitted red-and-green scarf, I breathe a sigh of relief. "Absolutely. Seems like a perfect day for *you* to enjoy."

Arti can't see me roll my eyes. I'm beginning to understand the human art of sarcasm. It's very similar to lying, so I'm not good at it and I don't plan on using it often. But it seems to fit today. The truth is, he will enjoy himself.

As we pass the laundromat, I'm reminded of my urgent need to do laundry. When my mother packed my trunk and suitcases for my departure from the North Pole, she thought of almost everything. I wish she could've given me self-cleaning clothes. After well over a hundred years of relying on elves to straighten my room, change my sheets, and provide me with laundered clothing, having to handle these tasks myself is the only downside of life in the human world.

Well, other than murder. That's not exactly something I've enjoyed experiencing.

We turn the corner toward Sven's sign shop, and the little open sign in the corner is visible.

Since he's generally in the back, working on orders, I let myself in and ring the bell on the counter. One ring only. I learned my lesson, after ringing out the entire chorus of "Jingle Bells" on a previous visit.

Sven rounds the corner, looking like an over-sized elf that just pulled a triple shift at Santa's toy factory.

"Hello, Mr. Tollesson. I thought you could use a friend."

He glances at the box in my hand. A weary grin peaks out from under his thick blond mustache. "Is that an apple dumpling?"

I wiggle the pastry box. "Even better. It's a gooey caramel cinnamon roll." He breathes a sigh of relief, steps forward, and accepts the gift.

The large treat is dwarfed in his huge bear paw. Sven devours the cinnamon roll and makes several satisfied sounds.

Waiting a moment for the sugary goodness to seep into his system, I amuse myself by gazing at the décor. No surprise that his entire shop is covered with signs.

"Are these all examples of your work or are some of them orders waiting to be picked up?"

His face warms with fatherly pride. "Some are examples of my work. Some are signs that were ordered and never picked up, and some — like these — are the handiwork of my oldest daughter, Linnéa."

"Wow. She's very talented. Even Santa's elves would be impressed with her woodworking skills."

My eyes widen, and I'm afraid to breathe. Naturally, Artikoa yips at my side — warning me of my blunder.

I've learned that raucous laughter is the best way to cover up a slip of the tongue.

Sven instantly believes I've made a silly joke and chuckles along with me. The combination of sugar and laughter finally lightens his spirit.

"I suppose you're here to grill me about this Ronnie business."

Stepping closer to the giant of a man, I look up and make sure my expression conveys how much I trust him. "Actually, I was hoping you could tell me something that would help me find the person who actually did this. I know you were upset. But I honestly don't believe you would hurt Ronnie."

Sadness and relief fill his eyes in equal measure.

"Thank you. You're the first person to say that to me. And, for what it's worth, I don't think you would hurt him either."

I hadn't realized anyone still considered me a suspect, but his words are reassuring. "Thank you. Let's work together to figure out what really happened."

He reaches out his large and somewhat sticky paw. "Deal."

Grabbing it without hesitation, I give it a firm shake. I've learned that humans are fairly obsessed with this handshaking gesture. All I ever wanted to do was fit in, so I shake every hand I get the opportunity to shake.

"Why don't you tell me what happened, Sven? You'll feel better." I take a seat on a rickety metal stool and wait.

Sven's behemoth shoulders slump, and his bearded chin drops to his chest as he collapses onto a worn-out plaid couch. The low sofa creaks in protest. He resembles a forlorn yeti.

"Shouldn't have gotten so upset. I know that now. Ronnie has never been the same since he lost Connie, God rest her. When you opened that bakery . . . Having somebody make her recipes again . . . It's the happiest I've seen him since she passed."

Spontaneous joy pushes up my cheeks, and I hope the light in my eyes will encourage him.

"When I heard he was leaving the bakery to you, I only thought about my financial problems and I didn't really think about Ronnie." Sven's deep-blue eyes peer up at me through his bushy blond eyebrows and dart away. "I wasn't thinking straight."

"It's okay, Sven. You and Mona are Ronnie's family. You deserve to inherit the bakery. I'd be happy to have you as my landlord. Don't give it a second thought." Leaning forward and softening my voice, I prod him once again. "What happened at the bar?"

"Welp, when I stormed outta your place, I went straight to The Shallows. Not proud of myself, but that's what happened. I sat down at the bar. Started drinking the hard stuff. Ol' Gunnar makes a mean apple pie moonshine."

My mouth turns down as I scrunch up my nose. I've never tasted moonshine, but if it's anything like the wine I drank at Betty Troup's, yuck. Sven catches sight of my expression, and, for the first time since I entered the sign shop, his wide beard quakes with laughter.

"That look on your face is spot on, Cindy. I had no business drinking that stuff. Anywhooo, Ronnie walked in and I pretty much lost it. I shouted at him about family first and keepin' his promises. I even threw in a nasty dig about what would Connie say?!" Sven's enormous hands cover his entire face and impressive beard.

"It's understandable. You were upset. What did Ronnie say?"

"He told me I should learn my place, respect my elders . . . buncha stuff like that. Ronnie told Gunnar not to breathe a word of it, and then he turned on a wooden nickel and marched out of the bar."

"Oh my! Well, that explains why Gunnar was so tight-lipped when I stopped in. Did Ronnie say where he was going?"

As Sven tosses his head back and forth, a loose tear takes flight.

Hopping off the stool, I place a comforting hand on his strong shoulder and squeeze. "It's not your fault. At least you and Ronnie didn't come to blows. That should count for something with the deputies, right?"

Sven swipes angrily at the tears, grabs a handkerchief from his back pocket, and blows his nose louder than an entire flock of Canadian geese. "If you say so, Cindy. Thing is, if I hadn't been so rude to him and chased him out of the bar—"

He doesn't need to finish the sentence. I can fill in the blank. If Ronnie hadn't left Shallow

Shoals so quickly, he wouldn't have been at his house when the attacker broke in. Did they break in? I don't remember what Keith said. What does he call it? Forced entry? I don't remember seeing any footprints in the snow — at least not heading to the front door.

"Thanks for listening to me, Cindy. I'm sure the deputies will be here to take me in any minute. That Winters fella musta told 'em about the argument. You should probably scoot. Not sure you want to be caught conspiring with a suspected criminal."

My heart cracks with sadness for this enormous man. Throwing my arms around his shoulders, my hands don't even meet in the back. I hug as tightly as I can, and offer my condolences.

He sniffles and exhales with a smidgen of relief.

"I'm going to head back to the bakery, Sven. If you or Mona need *anything*, you let me know. Right?"

He smiles, and it almost touches his eyes. "We will. Thanks for your friendship, eh?"

"No thanks necessary."

CHAPTER 8

*J*asmine left a little early to get ready for her date. Closing the bakery by myself reminds me of my first days in the human world — cleaning up this place with only Artikoa to keep me company. The smiling face of Ronnie walking in and promising me Connie's cookbooks . . . It won't be the same without him.

A chill passes through me, and the pages in Connie's cookbook flutter of their own accord. When the motion stops, I swallow loudly and walk toward the book.

The recipe showing is for peanut butter blossom cookies with a chocolate candy center.

"Connie? Is that you?" The room is so icy I can see my breath.

Nothing visible happens.

"I make these, but I use—" At that exact moment, a bag of miniature Santa Claus chocolates falls from the supply shelf.

That can't be a coincidence. My papa says there's no such thing.

"Connie, it has to be you. I'm so sorry about what happened to Ronnie. I'm doing everything I can to figure out who did this to him. I know it wasn't Sven."

A ladle rolls off the stove and clatters onto the floor. "I'll take that as agreement." As I stoop to collect the utensil, my gaze hits a gap in my bakeware.

"Hey, one of my ten-inch round baking pans is missing."

The chill seems to swirl around me.

A quick check of the pans in the drying rack reveals nothing. "Curling elf boots! How did I lose a pan?"

My breath leaves a frosty trail in the air.

"Sorry, I got sidetracked, Connie. Keith Winters has promised to keep me informed about the investigation. I'll look at some things, too. I'm going to find out who did this to your husband. I promise."

The chill in the air warms a few degrees, and, for a moment — could be my imagination — the face of Connie Schmenkel seems to float in front of me.

An agitated yip from the foyer reminds me I've locked Artikoa out of the bakery.

"Coming! Sorry I locked you out, Arti."

When I get to the door, there's a strange man standing in the foyer. The medium-sized human has a bandana tied around his stringy brown hair, and there's a tattoo covering his neck and snaking under the bandana.

Arti is on the steps with his hackles raised, and I'm frozen in place. There's something mildly familiar about the symbol on the man's shirt, but I can't place it. I don't think I should open the door.

As I reach into the pocket of my apron, my heart thumps in my chest, and I know beyond a shadow of a doubt he is on the Naughty List. Now I definitely don't know what to do.

Speaking loudly, so the man can hear me through the door, I offer an apology. "Sorry, we're closed. We open tomorrow morning at 6:00 a.m."

A flash of anger ruffles his features, and he throws his hands in the air. "Hey, I left my keys on my table over there. I work right across the street. Can't you just let me in to grab my keys?"

I glance over my shoulder and see a small ring of keys on the table in the corner. "Are you Oswald?"

He rolls his eyes. "Yeah. That's my last name. I'm the dishwasher over at D'lish." He points to the faded root-vegetable logo on the shirt peeking from under his stained jacket.

Hmmmm. If Zahara is willing to give him a second chance, suppose I should, too. Fishing the keys out of the pocket of my apron, I unlock the door and fumble with an apology. "Sorry about that. The shirt looked familiar. I couldn't quite place you. After what happened to Ronnie—"

Oswald's eyes narrow, and his lip curves up in a snarl. "Don't mention that guy around me." He pushes past me, retrieves his keys, and exits without so much as a thank you.

As soon as the exterior door closes behind him, my bossy fox lights into me.

"Cynthia Cherubim Claus, I can't have you ignoring my warnings. That man is dangerous. You heard how he spoke about Mr. Schmenkel. What if he's the killer?"

An icy hand seems to grip my spine. I hadn't thought about that. I'm definitely too trusting for this human world, but no need to give Arti the upper hand. "If Zahara can trust him enough to give him a second chance, I'm happy to follow suit. He may be on the Naughty List for now, but people can change their fate." Crossing my arms over my chest, I huff loudly.

Arti rests on his haunches, and his fluffy tail sweeps away my comment. "You are right about that minor detail. I have known humans to move themselves from the Naughty List to the Nice. But I have also seen the opposite, and, worst of all, I've witnessed those on the Naughty List make eternally grave decisions. You must be more careful. Do I make myself clear?"

"Yes." My voice trails off, and I look at the floor.

"Yes what?"

"Yes, most venerable Elder."

The proud arctic fox hums with satisfaction. "Now, let's lock up and get some rest."

"Rest? You must be kidding." Locking the bakery door and the exterior door, I turn and march up the steps, calling over my shoulder as I go, "There's no way I can rest while Ronnie's killer walks free. I'm going to see if Keith has any new information."

At the top of the steps, I approach the door on the left and knock lightly.

No reply.

If Keith were home, he'd definitely answer.

Ignoring Artikoa's smug chuckle, I open the door to our apartment, toss my apron on the floor, and poke through the icebox in search of supper.

Nothing looks good.

Loss of appetite is an entirely new experience for me.

As my eyes rove across my small apartment, it looks as though a mini indoor blizzard has hit. Practically everything I own is strewn about the place. I hadn't noticed what a mess it had become. Did it look like this when Keith was here?

"Oh dear. I think it's time to do laundry, Arti."

He lifts his judgmental nose in the air and says nothing.

Blizzards! That fox is pushing his enchanted luck.

Suited up in my last clean sweater, I grab my cute reindeer purse and unsnap Rudolph's red nose to make sure the zippered compartment is loaded with quarters. As I reach for the door handle — heaped basket in hand — there's a soft knock on my apartment door.

"Who is it?"

"It's Keith. I didn't wake you, did I? I know you have to get up early for the bakery."

Dropping the basket of my unsavory castoffs with a thud, I kick it toward the corner as I yank the door open. "Hi. Asleep? No. Not me."

Keith's trained investigative eye glances at my small purse and the heaping basket of clothing in the corner.

"Hey, I can catch up with you tomorrow. I'm sure you almost never have time to do your wash."

My shoulders slump with disappointment. "Yeah, it's not a habit I'm really used to. I'm happy Todd keeps the place open twenty-four hours a day, though. That makes it a little easier."

Keith steps back and tilts his head. "You know what? I need to do a couple of loads myself. Plus, I'll feel better knowing you aren't wandering around alone after dark."

My eyelashes flutter abnormally. "You worry about me?"

He steps toward his apartment and replies over his shoulder. "Definitely right now. We need to catch whoever did this to Ronnie. Let me grab my supplies, and I can bring you up to speed on the case while we wait."

Artikoa steps closer and whispers in an extremely quiet tone. Human ears would have no hope of catching his warning. "Do not involve yourself with humans."

Choking on my laughter, my brain spins to cover up the mistake. "I really do need to do laundry. Thanks. I'll be downstairs."

Keith reappears before I even have a chance to lock my door.

"Ready."

Slipping the keys into my purse, I turn and

stare at his perfect and pristine laundry hamper. His has a lid, and it's not propped open by mountains of filthy clothing. He carries nothing else in his hands, so I assume he must have his laundry detergent and stash of quarters tucked inside there as well. As I stoop to pick up my catastrophe of clothing, a familiar flush rushes up my neck and over my cheeks.

Keith glances at my attire. "I get the black leggings with white snowflakes, but I've never seen you wear a black sweater. And what kind of monster is embroidered on the front? That doesn't seem to have anything to do with your usual Christmas theme."

He leads the way downstairs and holds the front door for me.

"Actually, it has a lot to do with Christmas. That's Krampus. He's part of the German legends of the holiday. They have a little more of a punishment-based holiday system. St. Nicholas brings good girls and boys presents, and Krampus is rumored to punish or even — eat bad girls and boys. I've had this sweater since my goth-elf phase in my nineties."

"Yip. Yip."

The moment I hear the canine retribution, my enormous slip of the tongue hits me like an avalanche.

Keith snickers as we walk down the snowy sidewalk, heads tucked low against the wind.

"I love your sense of humor, Cindy. The '90s!" He snorts. "As if you were even alive, then. Well, I guess maybe you were born in the '90s. But, seriously! You couldn't be a day over twenty-five. Convince me I'm wrong." His twinkling eyes catch mine, and the heat that speeds from my toes to my head and back down again pushes away any hint of winter. There is no half-truth that will fix the situation.

He takes a deep breath and continues, "Goth-elf, you say? Never heard of that particular subset. My career in law enforcement has certainly gotten me face-to-face with a variety of things I never suspected about humanity. Most of them are disappointing, unfortunately. But I've never met a Gothic elf. I'm intrigued."

Maybe I should keep my half-elf, one-quarter-human, one-quarter angel mouth zipped for a bit.

The four-and-a-half-block walk to the laundromat is crisp and magical. The winter sky is frosty black and bursting with twinkling stars. The moon must be in its new phase, as none of its silvery light disturbs the celestial display.

CHAPTER 9

*B*right fluorescent lighting inside the laundromat offers a harsh greenish greeting. One long tube just inside the doorway flickers to a rhythm all its own. Keith points and shakes his head. "I wish I knew where Todd kept the replacements. I'd be happy to swap that one out for him." He heads over to a row of washing machines and opens two units.

"I don't think Todd would want you messing with them. He doesn't seem to like anyone poking around the laundromat. It's kind of a get in, do your wash, and get out scenario."

I walk to the six machines backing Keith's and select four washers. As I transfer items into a quartet of machines, I uncover some of my delicates. My eyes dart toward Keith, and his gaze flies toward the blinking light bulb.

"Maybe I'll run upstairs and knock on Todd's door. I'm sure he won't mind some help."

Keith starts the last of his machines and hurries out of the laundromat like a wolf sprung from a trap.

I toss items as fast as I possibly can, determined to empty my basket before he returns.

As I'm dropping quarters in and pushing the slide to activate the second machine, raised voices catch my attention.

Less than thirty seconds later, Keith reenters the laundromat, shaking his head in disbelief. "Not what I expected. I should've taken your advice. Turns out, Todd is not someone who appreciates assistance. He told me to mind my own business and finish doing laundry or he'd ban me from the establishment."

It's probably rude to laugh, but it spills forth before I can stop it.

Keith takes it in stride and moves his hamper on the floor. "Laugh all you want. I deserve it. You gave me fair warning."

"I did. I still feel bad that Todd yelled at you, though. You were only trying to help."

Keith heads toward the vending machine. "No

good deed goes unpunished, they say. Can I get you a snack?"

As the rushing water pouring into six machines fills the room with a wall of sound, Artikoa moves close. "I'm going to have a quick run. Maybe a hunt. I'll be back before your laundry is finished. Mind your manners with this human."

"Yes, MVE."

Arti's ears squeeze to even sharper points, and his wise gaze narrows. His loud exhale as I open the door for him reveals he's cracked my code. *Most Venerable Elder.* I didn't feel like saying it. I think the acronym works.

"Are you sure your dog will be all right out there alone? It's pretty cold tonight."

"He'll be fine. Thanks." If only he knew. "And in response to your question about a snack, I'm not really hungry. But if you buy a box of those little colorful chocolate candy bits. I might have a few."

"Okey dokey."

The ancient orange plastic chairs backing up to the front window are a far cry from comfortable, but the company makes almost anything tolerable.

Keith takes a seat next to me in one of the stiff chairs and angles his chin toward the churning machines. "How about we try to get to know each other a little better while we wait for our wash cycles to end?" He shakes the box and drops some of the brightly coated candies into my ready hand.

Oh boy. I could really use the interference of a certain bossy fox right about now. "Sure. Okay."

He leans back in the chair and rests his strong chin in the V of his hand as he taps his right cheek with an index finger. "Let's see. I'll start with a softball question. That's how I tend to run an interrogation. What's your full name?"

Whew. No problem. I can easily answer this one. "Cynthia Cherubim Claus."

One eyebrow tugs upward at an amusing angle as he evaluates my answer. "Interesting. And are you related to the most famous Claus of all?"

Looks like the so-called softball questions have ended. "I most certainly am." My lips quiver, and I attempt to lift the corners, but not much is accomplished.

Keith places his hands on his knees and rubs them back and forth. "Makes sense. It's not a very common name." He turns his head and sniffs once. "Okay. Your turn."

"Where did you live before you came to Silver Shoals?"

"Good question. Right before, I was in the Birch County Sheriff's Academy. Prior to that I was attending university in Chicago, to get my degree in forensic science. Ever since I was a kid, I knew I wanted to be involved in law enforcement and medicine. When I found out there was something called a medical investigator, I flipped, you know? It was my two favorite things smashed together. Like a peanut butter and mayonnaise sandwich."

Not having a clear view of my face, I don't know exactly how wide my eyes fly open, but it's enough to make Keith chuckle and add a hint of color to his cheeks.

"It's not that weird, is it? My mom worked a lot when I was a kid. I invented that sandwich, and I'm pretty proud of it."

Leaning forward, I touch his knee without thinking. "No, no. Just because I haven't heard of it before doesn't mean anything. I barely know anything about hu— huge sandwich trends." Twitching elf ears! That was close. I almost said "humans" out loud.

Keith lays his hand on top of mine, and a bolt of lightning flies up my arm, initiating the signature Claus rosy cheeks.

"Huge sandwich trends? I don't know if I'm familiar with any huge sandwich trends either. As far as I know, I'm the only one who eats that crazy combination."

I slide my hand out from under his and swipe at my throat, desperately searching for the voice that ran for cover. "Um, I . . ." It's barely a squeak. Taking a shallow breath, I make a second attempt. "You'll have to make one for me sometime. I'm sure it's delicious."

The surge of Keith's machines comes to a stop, and he glances toward the row of appliances. "It's definitely not as tasty as anything you make. But hold that thought. Let me get my stuff transferred over to some dryers, and we'll continue this game."

As he walks away, the heat in my cheeks lessens, and I'm able to draw a full breath. He thinks this is a game? I feel as though I'm walking the gangplank on a fictional pirate ship! If this is a game, I am sorely uninformed about the rules. I've got to remember to talk to Jasmine tomorrow.

My worries are interrupted, as my machines shut down one by one. "My turn."

While I transfer the laundry into the dryers, I catch Keith watching me. His expression is filled with something like admiration, but there's a layer beneath that's unfamiliar to me. Maybe I'll try to reach out to Mama through the snow globe. This could be one of those things she tried to explain to me when I was younger, and I simply couldn't grasp it.

Dropping a quarter through the slot and

pressing start on the last dryer, I turn and, before my personal pride can show on my face—

Todd yanks open the door and stomps in. "Are you two about done causing all the racket down here?"

I'm kinda squishy under pressure, and I have never been a fan of openly expressed anger. On the other hand, Keith takes it all in stride.

"Hey, Todd, I meant to tell you how much it means to those of us at the sheriff's station that you keep this place open 24/7. We get tied up with calls and the business of protecting this community at all hours. Being able to pop in here and get our uniforms and personal clothing cleaned any time of the day or night is a big help. It means a lot to the guys and gals on the force. You can be sure we make extra patrols in this area purely out of gratitude."

In keeping with my pirate-ship analogy, the boisterous north wind that had Todd's sails straining suddenly ceases, and the sheets hang limp as he shifts his weight from one foot to the other. "Appreciate that, Deputy Winters. I'm only trying to catch up on my sleep, you know. You two finish up and have a good night, eh?"

Keith stands and pats him firmly on the shoulder. "You betcha, Mr. Freeman. And we'll definitely keep it to a dull roar down here."

I swear to you, there's a seed of a smile poking out of the corner of Todd's mouth as he turns to head back to his upstairs apartment.

"Wow. You're sort of great with people. I didn't know what to say. He seemed so angry."

He saunters toward me. "Thanks. One of my instructors wanted to push me into hostage negotiation, but my obsession with pathology couldn't be satisfied by words alone."

The idea of someone enjoying examining dead bodies grips the back of my neck like a mama polar bear moving her cubs. "You — actually like examining the bodies?"

Keith bites his bottom lip and tips his head from shoulder to shoulder. "That's definitely not a softball question. Let's press pause on the game and talk about the case." He presses his pointer finger on an invisible button, and continues, "Did you find out anything interesting today?"

My first instinct is guilt. Strange. "Did Sven tell you I spoke to him?"

Keith's expression is relaxed and free of judgment. "He did. Said he was relieved that at least one person in town believed in his innocence."

"You don't think he's innocent?"

"Didn't say that. I'm not convinced either way. He only remains a person of interest, you know? However, as far as motive goes, stopping

Ronnie from changing the will is a pretty solid one."

"It wasn't Sven. I'm sure. But it has to be somebody who knew Mr. Schmenkel, right? They knew where he lived."

Pulling the little candies from my pocket, I push them around the palm of my hand. Sorting them into rows by color, I pop one in my mouth and it tastes of sadness.

Rather than answer my question, Keith twists in his chair to face me. "Are you okay? I've never known you to turn your nose up at sweets."

He tosses a handful of candies into his own mouth and patiently waits for my reply.

Switching gears to sorting the candies by quantity, I create a lopsided pyramid in my palm. "I've sort of lost my appetite since — you know."

He picks the candies from my palm one by one and places them back in the box. "No pressure. It's a very common response. You had a traumatic experience. The fact that you're pushing yourself to keep the bakery open is amazing. I'm sincerely glad you're planning on closing for at least a couple days. You need a break."

"Yeah. I guess I do." A sigh of relief escapes, and I press my back into the unwelcoming chair. "Ronnie was so kind to me. Bailing me out, with the whole Betty fiasco. The cookbooks — everything. It was the sweetest thing for him to offer to give me the bakery. I would much rather have him alive as my landlord than—" Silent tears trickle down my cheeks, and Keith reaches out and gently pats my knee.

"The only person responsible for what happened to Ronnie is the killer. There's nothing you or anyone else could've done. You're simply the one who found him. We're doing everything we can." He leans closer. "I promise you, I'm going to find the person who did this to Ronnie."

I wipe the tears from my cheeks and place my wet hand on top of his. "Thank you."

A moment of warm understanding hangs between us.

Keith presses for more information. "Did you find anything strange in your conversation with Sven?"

"Not really. I didn't know he was such a drinker, but just because it doesn't appeal to me . . ."

He nods. "Yeah. Sounds like he's under a lot of stress right now. Business isn't great, and he's got all those mouths to feed at home. It's not an ideal situation. I wish he had a better alibi. Sleeping one off at the sign shop with no witnesses and no one to vouch for him isn't great."

"Are there any other suspects?"

Keith sniffs sharply. "Sadly, there are hundreds. Ronnie was a force to be reckoned with when he was a deputy. He solved more cases than any sheriff's deputy in the history of Silver Shoals. His record still stands today."

Scrunching up my nose, I turn toward him. "Sounds like a good thing. He was taking care of the community. Wasn't he?"

Keith's head bobs rapidly, and he rakes a hand through his dark hair. "Yeah, for sure. For sure. Problem is, for every one of those cases he solved, it means a criminal went to jail. And convicts are the kind of people who hold grudges. Deputy Rivera has a couple officers going through Ronnie's old case files right now. We're looking for any red flags. Threats. Guys who got extra time tacked onto their sentences because of specific evidence or testimony that Ronnie may have supplied. It's a pretty long list. A lot of them are still in the pen, but the deputies might turn something up. You never know."

"I never thought of that. Seems like putting bad people where they belong is a good thing. Can't imagine people being upset about that."

Keith twists his neck and stares at me. "Didn't you have criminals where you came from? Seems to me they are a universally bad breed."

Gulp. "Oh, sure, sure. Makes sense." Before I can make a bigger muskox of myself, a paw scratches at the glass door.

"Arti! You're back. Do you have any news?"

Ignoring my all-too-human question, Artikoa brushes past me and yips below one of the dryers.

"Oh look. My clothes are done. I'll grab everything and deal with folding tomorrow."

As I stuff hot laundry into my basket, Keith follows suit.

We stroll home in silence, but our shoulders brush dramatically three times before we get to our walkup and trudge upstairs.

On the landing between our apartments, he turns. "G'nite, Cindy." He shakes the half-empty box of candies. "Should I save these for you?"

"No thanks. You go ahead." As I fumble for my key, Artikoa paces between us and eyes Keith with intense judgment.

"Yip."

"Arti, that's enough. Keith is a good friend and an excellent laundry buddy." Shoving open the door to my apartment with the laundry basket, I press my luck. "Now, get in the apartment and no more barking."

Artikoa slinks past me and gazes upward. If looks could turn me into an iceberg . . .

Keith chuckles.

"Thanks for keeping me company, Keith. Goodnight."

The last thing I feel is the tummy-tingling warmth beaming from his smile as he closes his door.

CHAPTER 10

*P*ausing at the top of the stairs, I listen with my ultra-sensitive elf hearing and discern nothing stirring within Keith's apartment. Odd. I didn't hear him leave this morning.

Artikoa and I descend to find Jasmine hard at work prepping coffee for the day.

"Good morning, Jazz. I'm about to start the day's baking. You're here early."

"Totally. I couldn't sleep, or whatever. Figured I might as well be here." Her back is turned, but her voice has a grumpy edge.

"Sorry you didn't get a good night's sleep. I think the whole thing with Ronnie has us all worried." I grab a previously worn green apron from the hook and tie it around my waist. There's a faint smudge of flour from yesterday, but I can get one more use out of it.

Jasmine turns and cradles an enormous mug in both of her talented hands. "Yeah. Like, I didn't know the guy. But it's weird, right? I've never really known anyone who's kicked it."

Relying on my growing knowledge of slang, I'm comfortable assuming "kicked it" means dead.

"Are you sure you're okay to work today?"

Jasmine lifts her narrow shoulders, and they drop with a bounce. "Sure. What else am I gonna do?"

Inhaling slowly, I let my mind wander over my options. "Tell you what, I'll grab everything for this morning and get the cases filled. Then I'm going to take a batch of cranberry orange scones down to Sven. Will you be okay on your own?"

She glances around the absolutely empty coffee shop, and a smirk lightens her weary face. "I think I can handle it, boss."

Heading into the back room, I quickly transfer trays of delicious treats to the display case. Last but not least, I arrange a fresh batch of apple dumplings in the glass-dome-covered cake stand. The sight of them brings visions of Ronnie to my head.

After wiping an errant tear, I remind Jasmine to heat them up in the toaster oven if anyone asks.

"Sure." She nurses her enormous caffeinated beverage like an abandoned baby reindeer on a bottle.

"I'm going to pop the scones in the oven to give them a quick warm-up, and then I'll head down to the sign shop. I shouldn't be gone more than forty-five minutes."

She offers me a wide yawn and a silent nod.

Alone in the back room, I'm reminded of my missing pan. "Jazz, have you seen a ten-inch round anywhere?"

Her sleepy blue eyes peer around the corner. "Not that I know of? Why?"

"One's missing." My shoulders pinch with concern.

"I'll keep an eye out, boss." She slinks out of sight.

WITH THE SCONES WRAPPED in two layers of clean cloth dishtowels and tucked in a basket, I trade my apron for a toasty winter jacket and hurry down the street.

As I round the corner, the "Open" sign is still turned to "Closed." Approaching with caution, I knock firmly. Something tells me Sven is inside.

Wrong. No one answers.

Gazing at my basket of scones in disappointment, I turn to leave.

The door creaks open behind me, and, when I glance over my shoulder, I'm not sure if I'm looking at a bedraggled grizzly or a terribly unhappy man. "Sven?"

He rubs an enormous paw across his reddened face. "You woke me up. What's all this about?"

Before I can answer, a car pulls into the parking lot, and a freshly shaved Keith Winters steps out — taking in the strange scene as he approaches. "How are you now, Mr. Tollesson?"

Rather than answer, Sven lowers his head, exhales loudly, and gestures for us to enter.

He offers me the rickety stool, and he collapses onto the dilapidated sofa tucked behind the counter. Keith is right at home, standing between us. "Sven, I need to ask you some more questions. Would you like Cindy to leave?"

Mr. Tollesson takes a quick whiff toward my basket. "Nah. Cindy's good people. And I want to know what she's got in that basket."

Passing the basket to Keith, I explain as it makes its way toward Sven. "Those are cranberry orange scones. I warmed them up this morning. But technically, I made them yesterday. Didn't have time to make fresh. Sorry about that."

Sven takes the basket and unwraps the pastries, as though he's taking his first peek at a newborn. "No need to apologize, there. These smell like a little slice of heaven." He grabs two and passes the basket back to Mr. Winters. "Help yourself, Deputy."

Keith takes one and tips the basket my way. I shake my head and wave the food away. My appetite is still nonexistent.

He enjoys a bite or two of scone before proceeding with his interview. "These are absolutely delicious, Cindy. I'm glad I arrived when I did."

Sven mumbles through his nearly full mouth. "Ten minutes from now, they'd all be gone."

This comment brings a surprising chuckle from all present.

"Now, Sven, I want you to know, these are routine questions." Keith pauses and drops his chin. "Please answer honestly. I'm doing the best I can over here to find additional evidence."

Sven bobs his head once as he continues to chew.

"We found your prints at the scene."

Mr. Tollesson chokes on what remains of his scone as he waves a hand in objection, but Keith motions for him to simmer down.

"Don't worry. I know you and your family were regular visitors to Ronnie's home. I expected to find your prints all over the place. Thing is, the only place we didn't find your prints was on that rolling pin."

The stool beneath me squeaks in protest as I lean forward. "That's great. That means he's off the suspect list. Right?"

Keith sniffs sharply and shakes his head once. "I wish it were that easy. The issue is we didn't find *any* prints on the rolling pin except yours, Cindy. That means the killer likely wiped it clean and planted your prints, as I explained before. I was really hoping there'd be another print or two on there that would clear both of you."

I'm on my feet in an instant. My voice is louder than intended. "Wait! I'm still a suspect? That's ridiculous."

Sven chimes in. "At the risk of bloodying my own nose, I've gotta agree with Cindy. You and I both know there's no way a sweet girl like her did this, Winters."

"It's not about what I think. It's about what the evidence can prove. I know we're all friends here, but that can't play into my investigation. I've gotta find hard evidence that leads to Ronnie's killer. Right now I don't have anything that lets me rule the both of you out completely. I'm still following every lead." A crease darkens his brow. "Trust me. I want to find the actual culprit, and not just close the case for the sake of Deputy Rivera's annual report." Keith throws his arms in the air, and his frustration is palpable.

As I lower myself onto the old stool, a light blinks on in my head as brightly as when my mama used to wave her hands to bring Ol' Tannenbaum to life at the North Pole. "Hey, what about the stand on the shelf?"

Sven and Keith gaze at me as though I've lost all my jingle bells.

"What are you talking about, Cindy?" Keith steps closer and momentarily overheats my system.

After taking a steadying breath, I explain. "The first time I visited Mr. Schmenkel's house, he showed me that rolling pin. He was as proud of it as he was of the recipe books he'd passed along. Ronnie asked me if I wanted it, and I told him I thought it should remain at his house. In a place of honor."

Keith's eyes show a glint of understanding, but a tight smile hints at impatience. "Okay. Is there more to the story?"

"Oh! Yes, of course. When he lifted the rolling pin, the metal stand that held it kind of stuck to the handles. He mumbled something like, 'That darn thing never fit in there right,' and he had to hold it down with one hand and pull the rolling pin free with the other. Whoever grabbed that rolling pin might've thought to wipe it clean, but they probably forgot they'd touched the other piece."

Keith grabs his mobile telephone from a pocket inside his jacket. There's no need for him to explain how brilliant I am. The pride in his voice is clear as he relays this new information to Deputy Rivera. "So we better get somebody out there to dust that stand for prints ASAP. The last thing we want is the murderer returning to the scene of the crime to destroy evidence."

He ends the call and glances from me to Sven and back again. "I've got everything I need, for now. If this new lead pans out, I should be able to clear both of you by the end of the day." He hands the basket of scones to me as he passes. "The deputies would sure love it if you brought a box of these into the station. They've been working some long hours, going over Ronnie's old case files."

Keith lets himself out, and I walk toward Sven to set the basket on his sagging blue sofa.

"Oh, I've had my fill, Cindy. My appetite isn't what it used to be. This whole mess with Ronnie has got my stomach in knots, you know?"

"I absolutely know. Mind if I take the rest of these over to the station?"

Sven looks up at me, and his eyes are filled with gratitude. "I'm starting to think you're my guardian angel, Cindy. Go ahead and do whatever you think is best with those scones. I sure hope you're right about that stand."

With one hand I grab the basket, and with the other, I cross my fingers and shake them in his direction. As I leave, he yawns with the gusto of a wild creature and collapses onto the couch.

CHAPTER 11

The sheriff's station is all abustle. It reminds me of the busy elves in my father's factory. A fresh twinge of homesickness squeezes my heart.

News of Keith's new lead is spreading like hot gossip in a small town — or so I've learned.

Looking toward a dented metal desk in the corner, I feel happiness in my heart as I glance at the deputy's badge. Deputy Chrisp is definitely on the Nice List.

"Can I offer you a cranberry orange scone?"

Her head lifts, and she blinks twice, as though she's hoping she's not seeing a mirage. "You betcha. This running through old cases is purely mind-numbing. I could use a little pick-me-up."

As my eyes flick from paper to paper on the officer's desk, I'm once again filled with wonder for the late Ronnie Schmenkel. "These are all the cases he solved?"

"Hard to believe, isn't it? I can't believe we ever had this much crime. But he was on the force thirty-five years. I guess anybody would get close to cracking four hundred cases with that kind of time under their belt."

"Four hundred! How can you possibly look into that many suspects?"

She sighs. "Welp, it's a process of elimination, really. First step is looking at anybody who's still in the clink. That takes 'em off the list right away. Then we look for anybody who's no longer with us. I figure if they've crossed over, they can't be causin' this kind of trouble."

Her assumption brings to mind Connie Schmenkel's ghost. So far, that ghost has only been helpful. What if she was somehow angry or vengeful? I definitely need to talk to my mama. I don't know anything about ghosts. "Well, how many does that leave?"

The young deputy wipes a hand across her smooth brow. "That still leaves us with a hundred and twenty suspects. Now, some of these crimes weren't too serious, so I've moved all of those files to a pile over there. The ones who were in for any sort of violent crime and are out on parole or served their time. That's this bunch here."

Glancing at the thick stack of papers, my heart thuds heavily. "Gosh, that still looks like over sixty names."

Deputy Chrisp pauses, her scone hovering in midair. "It's exactly sixty names. Are you one of those math savants?"

"Me? Oh, no. Just real good with lists. As a matter of fact, people tell me I have an excellent intuition about folks. I bet if you let me take a look at that pile, I could cut it in half in no time."

The strain of the last twenty-four hours spent staring at nothing but paperwork whispers from the lines around Chrisp's hazel eyes. "Well, you're a civilian. I can't do anything official, you know." She looks around the station at her preoccupied compatriots. "Tell you what, why don't you give me that basket and I'll make the rounds? I can't be held responsible for what happens when I'm not at my desk."

She scoops up the basket and walks away. My experience with subterfuge is immensely limited. However, I get the feeling in my bones that she's giving me permission.

Grabbing the stack of sixty possibilities, I divide them into Naughty and Nice as fast as my hands can go.

I'm surprised to find so many Nice in the pile. Maybe some folks do learn the hard way. Mama always said I was one of those. As the last sheet flutters onto the Naughty pile, Deputy Chrisp returns with the empty basket. "Here you go, Miss. Anything I should know?" She gestures to the two piles of files. I point to the larger stack. "Nice." And then the smaller pile. "Naughty." She tilts her head and scrunches up her nose as though she smells a rotten apple. "Welp, better start with the Naughty List. Wouldn't you say?"

Picking up the basket, I offer her a wink and a nod.

Between the possibility of fingerprints on the rolling pin stand and a now shorter list of suspects, I feel as though I've put a real dent in this case today. Best hustle back to the bakery and see if Jasmine needs any help.

Traffic is light when I open the main door, and Artikoa races down from the apartment before I can take a step toward the bakery.

"You're needed urgently in the apartment."

"What?"

"Yip. Yip."

Two of my regulars walk out of the bakery with large coffees and to-go bags. I flash a hasty grin and wave to the ladies as I rush up the stairs.

Once inside the apartment, I see the issue immediately. My precious snow globe depicting the North Pole is pulsing like a beacon.

Pressing my hand to the cool glass surface, I instantly see the face of my mother. "Cynthia, are you in danger?"

"Me? I don't think so. What's going on?"

"I received word from a puffin, who heard it from an arctic hare, who received a message from an osprey, who overheard two polar bears—"

"Mama! I don't need to hear the whole chain of the gossip. What have you heard?"

"My sources tell me you've been accused of murder." Her shimmering green eyes narrow to slits, and her graceful arms cross heavily over her regal chest.

"Oh, that was nothing. A misunderstanding. It was days ago." My hands are waving wildly, and my mouth feels dry.

"It doesn't sound like nothing, Marshmallow. I can pop over in an instant if you need me to fix anything."

"No, Mama. I can handle it. I'm making my own way here. Death is part of living in the human world. We've got some good suspects, and I'm sure this whole matter will be cleared up before Christmas."

"I hope you're right, dear. I wouldn't want anything to ruin your father's visit. Your birthday is his favorite day of the year."

"Mama." We share a chuckle. "My birthday is on *Christmas*. I think it was his favorite day of the year long before I was born."

Golden sparkles swirl from my mother's hand, and, for a moment, it's as though her fingers gently brush my cheek. "I miss you every day, Marshmallow. You know you can come home anytime. The kingdom is here waiting for you. It wouldn't be a failure. It—"

My hand covers the swirl of warmth on my cheek. "I like it here, Mama. I'm making friends. I'm useful. And it's something that I built for myself."

The love and warmth dissipate as my mother lifts her chin. "Very well. Who is this human you were accused of injuring?"

"His name is Ronnie Schmenkel. My landlord. He wanted to give me the whole building, but he passed away before he could change his will. It's for the best, though. His cousin could really use the money more than me. I'm happy to keep renting and see how things go."

A shiver of regret and loss washes over me, and I rush to change the subject. "The bakery is a big success, Mama. Tell Cinnamon Roll, okay?"

My mother inhales sharply. "I shall pass along

your message. I do hope you are continuing to eat healthy and exercise. Remember, healthy holidays. That's our motto."

I don't have the heart to remind her it's only *her* motto.

"Mama, can you see ghosts?"

"Why on earth would you ask me that?" Her gaze narrows.

"The woman who had a bakery here before — Ronnie's wife — I think her ghost is still in the bakery." Swallowing with difficulty, I wait for her response.

"It must be the angel blood that allows you to see spirits of the deceased. I'm sure I have an old ritual around here somewhere that would exorcise her spirit from the build—"

"Oh, gosh no! I was hoping you could tell me how to communicate with her." My heart is racing and my breathing shallow.

"You *want* to talk to this apparition?" Mama's eyes fill with shock and the tiniest hint of admiration.

"Yes. She's helped me, or tried to, a couple of times. If I could understand her better . . ."

"Very well, my princess. I will research this matter. If I discover any aid, I will send it with your father." She leans away and studies me.

"I love you, Mama. I made something for you. I'll send it home with Papa."

Her eyes briefly fill with concern before waving her hand over the globe on her ornate desk. Mama's image vanishes, and my snow globe goes dark. Nothing more than decoration on the wooden table by my bedside.

Artikoa squirms on the plush green-velvet chair. Something in his mannerisms is suspicious.

"Arti, did you have anything to do with this rumor that raced through the wilderness?"

The elder statesman shifts his weight, fluffs his tail, and rests his pointed chin on the arm.

"Artikoa! I demand an answer. You may be here at my father's request, but I am Princess of the North Pole, and you answer to my family."

At the invocation of my regal heritage, the fox sits bolt upright. "I grew concerned for your well-being. These humans are too fragile. I'm not sure I can keep you safe in a place with so many dangers."

Kneeling down in front of the chair, I stroke the fur of his neck and let my voice hum with respect. "It's not your job to keep me safe. I chose this life, and I'm responsible for everything that happens here. Father wanted you to advise me. That doesn't make you responsible for my well-being."

The wise fox's true age mixes with the concern in his golden eyes. "Your father would be heartbroken if any harm came to you. I surmised from the moment we set foot in this world that advising was only a fraction of my true duty. I will lay down my life for you if necessary, Cynthia Cherubim Claus."

My voice catches in my throat, and tears fill my eyes. His devotion touches me deeply. What can I possibly say?

Drawing a shaky breath, I utter the only words I have. "Thank you."

CHAPTER 12

*T*he afternoon flies by faster than a flock of arctic terns headed south for winter. Before I know it, Jasmine is locking the bakery doors and turning the chairs up onto the table so she can sweep.

"Do you mind if I chat with you while you sweep?"

She pulls a curved white piece of plastic from her ear and shrugs. "No problem. I can jam out to my tunes later."

"Thanks. I wanted to ask you about the rules of dating." My nerves are causing my mouth to feel hot and my throat to tighten up.

"The rules of dating?" She shakes her deep-brown high ponytail. "I mean, the first rule is there are no rules. But that's me. We're about the same age. I'm sure you know what guys can be like."

I'm likely four or five times older than her, but that hardly matters. She has far more experience in this area. "My parents kept me super busy, and I couldn't really date. I think Keith Winters might be interested in me, but—"

"You think?" For some reason, this comment brings raucous laughter from Jasmine. "Keith is straight-up crazy about you, Cindy. I wish there was a guy who looked at me the way he looks at you."

My gaze falters, and prickling heat pinks up my cheeks. "Okay. So, he had coffee with me the other day, then he went and did laundry with me last night, and he wants to make me a sandwich. Is that a date?"

Jasmines stops sweeping and leans the broom against a nearby table. "Coffee. Laundry. Sandwiches. Did he try anything?"

I'm so flustered, I knock a napkin holder off the counter. It pops open and tree-shaped napkins flutter across the floor like a boreal apocalypse.

Jasmine giggles. "Oh, thanks. I already swept over there."

Hustling to scoop them up, I grab the napkin holder, but Jasmine puts her hand on top of mine. "You can't put them back in there. Like, once they touch the floor, they're considered unsanitary. That would be a health-code violation, so, like, the health inspector could shut you down."

I immediately release the napkin mess to Jasmine.

The health inspector. One of my least favorite people. My instincts told me he was on the Nice List, but everything about him screamed he should be on the Naughty. He was so cranky, and he spent hours here, poking and prodding and complaining about every little thing. Ronnie didn't think anything of it and easily helped me correct what he called minor issues. He said he and the health inspector had gotten into it when Connie was running her bakery. Sounded like a long-time rivalry.

"Well, I definitely don't want to make that guy angry. The less I have to see of him, the better."

Jasmine mumbles in agreement and tosses the napkins into the trash. "Did Keith kiss you?"

The amount of heat radiating from my face feels as though it could melt an iceberg. "Kiss? Oh no. He just drank the coffee with me at the corner table in the other room and went with me to do laundry."

Jasmine licks her lip and winks wickedly. "Watch out. Secret coffee *and* a trip to the laundromat. This guy's got your number, Cindy."

"Of course he has my number. I gave it to him when we were working on the Betty Troup case."

She rolls her eyes and ties up the trash bag. "Haven't you heard that saying before? It means he knows what you're into. Like, he knows how to get you interested. I think it's safe to say that if Keith asks you anywhere to do anything, it's totally a date."

Hefting the trash bag over her shoulder, she plods toward the back door. Following on her heels, I have more questions. "Do you think he's nice? He seems like a safe guy, right?"

Jasmine opens the door and launches the large black plastic bag into the dumpster. Wiping her hands on her red apron, she replies, "Keith? Keith is probably a saint. He hasn't lived in town long, but I've never heard a single bad thing about him. And trust me when I tell you, I am super plugged in."

She must be talking about the local gossip circuit. Even in my short time here, I've learned it is an incredibly effective means of spreading information — good and bad. "Okay. I definitely like him. Should I ask him to dinner?"

Jasmine closes the back door and throws the deadbolt. "Totally. I'm all for modern women asking for what they need. What have you got to lose?"

My stomach lurches, and its unusual emptiness sends a shock wave of nausea through my system. "I don't know. What if I ruin the friendship?"

"Look, Cindy, you're the whole package. You're a hottie, hella smart, and you own your business. Not to mention that wacky sense of humor. Any guy in this town would be lucky to break off a piece of that."

Once again, I've only understood half of what she's saying.

A yip outside the main doors of the bakery snaps me back to reality. "Thanks for cleaning up, Jazz. I'll see you tomorrow, and wish me luck. I'll see if Keith wants to go to dinner tonight."

She tosses her apron in the laundry hamper and offers me a thumbs up. "See you tomorrow, boss lady."

Now to run upstairs, and find a casual way to invite Keith to dinner.

Arti follows close on my heels, sniffing intrusively as I climb the staircase. "You are up to something. What is it?"

Thrilled to know something he doesn't, I offer a teasing reply. "You'll have to wait and find out."

I could make dinner, but I'm a far better baker than a cook. I love the potpie from D'lish. Maybe I can convince him to join me.

Now, to throw Artikoa off the scent. "I'm going

to grab dinner across the street. Can I offer you some chicken or coddled eggs before I leave?"

He prances into the kitchen and sits near the icebox. "Something about your mannerisms indicates you're in a hurry. If you place a generous portion of raw chicken in a bowl, I'll take care of myself."

"Thanks. I owe you one."

His head cocks to one side. "I was unaware we were keeping score. I shall review the ledgers while you're out. I feel you owe me more than one."

Anxiety has me knocking so lightly on Keith's door it seems impossible that he would hear. However, as I lift my fist to attempt something with more gusto, the door pops open.

Keith tilts his head back, and his lips curve in surprise. "How long have you been standing out there? I didn't hear you knock."

"Oh. I did. Just not very loudly. If you didn't hear me knock, why did you open the door?"

"I have to run across the street—"

"Me too! Do you want to have dinner?" Oops. I interrupted, and his expression looks somehow more confused than happy.

He grabs his keys from a small hook beside the door, spins them around his finger, and grins. "On one condition."

"What condition?"

"You let me buy you dinner."

"What? Oh no. I was inviting— Oh, dear. I have gotten this more tangled than a reindeer harness in a blizzard."

He laughs as he closes his door and pushes the key into the lock. "I have no idea how tangled that would be, but we're both hungry. What about going to the same restaurant? And I call dibs on paying the check."

"Okay. But you'll let me pay next time, right?"

His eyes dance with mischief, and he leans toward me. "I'm just glad to hear there'll be a next time." He abruptly sobers. "I do have to do a bit of work over there if that's all right?"

"Sure. That's okay."

After looking both ways, we hurry across the street and into the warm, spicy aromas of D'lish.

My first *official* date. How exciting!

CHAPTER 13

Keith makes a grand gesture of holding the door for me as we step inside the restaurant. His green eyes twinkle and he makes a slight bow. The natural wave in his swooped-back bangs keeps them neatly in place. The aroma of freshly baking bread swirls around us, and my tummy rumbles in hungry response. Finally! I have an appetite.

Zahara's tight, onyx-black curls bounce as she hurries toward the hostess podium. "Welcome! You two are just in time for my fresh bread! I had a run on sandwiches today and had to make six extra loaves after the lunch rush."

"Something definitely smells delicious." I rub my hands together in anticipation.

Zahara flashes a toothy grin. "That's high praise coming from you, Cindy. Are you guys ordering takeout, or can I get you a table?"

Keith leans forward and whispers conspiratorially, "Technically, we're not together. We happened to choose the same restaurant for dinner and, in a strange twist of events, I'm stuck paying both bills. You may as well seat us together."

She chuckles and arches a pierced eyebrow at me before taking us to a small table by the front windows. Pulling a lighter from the pocket of her lavender apron, she ignites the candle between us.

"Everything is on the menu tonight. I didn't have a chance to drum up a separate special, since I had to make the extra bread. But, I can tell you the chicken-less potpie is especially delicious today. I used the last of the Queensland blue pumpkins from Harlequin Crest Farms."

"Mm-mm. That sounds good to me." Keith offers her a pleasant bob of his head and motions for me to order.

"Make that two." I lick my lips in anticipation. "Oh, and if it's not too much trouble, I'd love a slice of fresh bread with extra butter."

Zahara tilts her head to Keith. "Same for you?"

"Absolutely."

"My pleasure." The skin around her eyes crinkles and her entire face exudes gratitude.

As she turns to leave, Keith reaches out and touches her arm. "Excuse me, Zahara. Would it be all right if I stepped in the back to have a quick chat with Bolton Oswald?"

"Bolton?" The mood changes faster than Santa can slide down a chimney. "Is he in some kind of trouble?"

Keith takes a deep breath and shrugs his shoulders. "Let's hope not. At this point, it's simply routine. I'll only be a minute."

She inhales sharply. "Follow me."

Our hostess leads him back to the dish room while I gaze into the candle flame, wondering if the details of the date will be something to share with Jasmine. Maybe it will even be something worthy of a snow-globe call to Mama.

Before any warm fuzzy feelings can take root, a commotion at the back of the restaurant draws my attention. Keith is backing up rapidly, while Bolton advances on him with one thick finger poking mercilessly into Keith's chest.

"So, that's how it's going to be, eh? I been outta the pen for almost six months. And I been keeping my nose clean . . . Checking in with my PO. But the first time anything goes wrong in your little town, must be the ex-con!"

The additional five patrons in the establishment have all twisted in their seats and are gawking at the display.

Zahara bursts from the kitchen, concern pinching her sharp features.

"Hey, guys, let's all simmer down. Okay?"

Bolton turns on her. "Is this the kind of establishment you run? You told me when you hired me you wouldn't judge me by my past screw-ups. What's this? You just let cops question all your employees?"

The color drains from Zahara's face, and her full lips make a series of silent shapes as she struggles for an appropriate response.

Getting to my feet, I foolishly rush toward the fracas. "I'm sure there's some misunderstanding—"

"You?" Bolton's eyes narrow. "You're Ronnie's pet, aren't you? You're probably the one who put this stupid idea in the cop's head."

The harshness in his tone causes me to take a physical step backward. "Me? No, I—" A flash of his name on one of the sheets of paper I sorted for Deputy Chrisp darts through my head. Technically, he's right. I put his sheet on the Naughty pile.

Keith steps between us. "Mr. Oswald, I asked you to stop by the station after your shift to answer a few questions. You're not under arrest. It wasn't even meant to be an official interrogation. However, your reaction is causing me to rethink things. Maybe a casual approach wasn't what was needed."

A dash of the mounting fury leaks out of Bolton's expression.

Keith taps a button on his phone and instantly takes decisive action.

While he places the call, I catch sight of a particularly interesting pan in the dish room. "Hey, that's my pan." Stepping forward, I grab a ten-inch round cake pan from the drying rack and show Zahara the engraving on the side. "Connie's Confections."

"Bolton, how did this get in our restaurant?" Zahara's eyes flash with anger and embarrassment. "Did you take this from Cindy's bakery?"

"What?" Bolton Oswald looks genuinely confused. "It says Connie. Why would it be at her place?" He juts an angry thumb in my direction.

Keith's official voice fills the momentary silence. "This is Winters. Send Chrisp over to D'lish to pick up the dishwasher, Bolton Oswald. Throw him in a cell until I get down to the station and have a chance to question him." He slips his phone back into his pocket and sizes up the suspect.

"Are we adding petty theft to the charges, Mr. Oswald?"

The dishwasher throws his wiry arms in the air and exhales. "I found that pan layin' on the sidewalk. It looked pretty good, so I brought it in an' scrubbed it. That a crime now?"

"Do you want to press charges, Cindy?" Keith waits patiently for my answer.

My head is buzzing with possible explanations. The last thing I want to do is make an enemy out of Bolton — if it's not too late. "No. No. Just glad to have the pan back. No charges."

Keith turns his attention back to the dishwasher. His tone is all business. "I'd advise you to step back into the dish room and collect your things. If you're not standing on the curb in five minutes, waiting for your ride with officer Chrisp, I'm going to add an 'assaulting an officer' charge to the list of things we'll be discussing at your interrogation."

Bolton's shoulders droop heavily, and the last sparks of his misplaced anger fizzle like a magic wand dropped into a punch bowl.

Keith returns to the table as though nothing has happened.

"How can you do that?"

"Do what?" The way his nose crinkles and eyebrows knit together brings a hint of amusement to my lips.

"You really are cool as an iceberg, aren't you?"

Sudden clarity dawns. He leans back and exhales slowly. "You mean the dustup with Mr. Oswald, right?" Keith grabs his napkin off the table, unfolds it, and places it in his lap. "I heard a saying when I was in college: 'What other people think of me is none of my business.' I've forgotten who said it, but it stuck with me. When suspects or perpetrators get defensive and lash out, I try to let it slide off like water off a duck's back." He inhales sharply. "It's not always easy. Sometimes they can make the attacks seem very personal. Truth is, I've lost my cool a few times."

His confession piques my interest. "Have you — ever — been in a fight?" Fights almost never occur at the North Pole. Even when they do, the negative energy quickly dissipates. Elves are natural problem solvers and rarely lose their tempers or, for that matter, hold grudges.

Keith sucks both of his cheeks in and wiggles his jaw back and forth. "That feels like a second-date question."

Heat rockets from my cheeks to my toes and back up again. "Okay." Pushing those two syllables past my lips is all I can manage.

He pauses, glances at the cake pan, and taps two fingers on his lips. "How long was this pan missing?"

"I'm not sure. I noticed it yesterday . . . or maybe the day before."

"Do you put the pans back in the storage racks or does Jasmine?"

I can't imagine what he's getting at. "Mostly me. I like things a certain way. Is that wrong?"

Keith's easy laughter releases the knot between my shoulder blades. "Not at all. Thing is, if you put the pans away, that pan would've had two or three nice, clean prints. Maybe Mr. Oswald copied those prints to create the fake set used to plant your prints on the rolling pin."

"Could he do that?" My mouth hangs open in shock.

"That robbery he was involved in, the one Ronnie put him away for, included bypassing a fingerprint ID alarm." Keith bobs his head and rubs a hand across his chin.

My heart thuds dangerously in my chest. Had Artikoa been right? Had I let a murderer into my bakery after hours?

Thankfully, Zahara pops out of the kitchen with a tray carrying our potpies. She balances the tray on one hand and expertly transfers the steaming ramekins to the table. "Careful, the dishes are hot."

My eyes widen at the welcome interruption, and I inhale the aromas. "Oh, that looks as good as it smells. Thank you."

She lowers her eyelids and her cheeks flush. "My pleasure."

As Keith and I work through our meals, it pleases me to note that we move at the same speed. Both of us are thoroughly enjoying our food, and neither of us is shy about consuming it with gusto. He pulls the napkin from his lap, wipes it across his lips, and sighs with satisfaction. "The only thing that could possibly top that meal would be a sweet treat from your bakery."

Taking a sip of cool water to calm my fluttering nerves, I attempt to meet him head-on. "Why don't we head over to my apartment? I'm sure I can rustle something up."

Mischief dances in his eyes for a moment and then vanishes like a candle in a windstorm. My spirits sink.

"Tell you what, Cindy. If you don't mind accompanying me down to the station first, I'll take you up on that offer."

"But I thought I wasn't a suspect anymore?"

Keith laughs out loud. "As far as I'm concerned, you never were. I'm not asking you to come down to the station for questioning. I'm asking you down so I can interview Mr. Oswald. In fact, if you'd like, I can set you up in the observation room and you can eavesdrop on the interrogation. How's that sound?"

I honestly can't imagine myself as a spy, but his offer is enticing enough to get my blood racing. "Gosh. That sounds fun."

As agreed, Keith pays our bill before we walk out to his car across the street. From the outside, the vehicle is a thoroughly nondescript grey sedan. However, from my vantage point in the front seat, I can see a variety of high-tech gear locked into brackets on the center console and wired into various parts of his dashboard.

"Is this a sheriff's vehicle?"

"For sure. This is standard issue for detectives and medical investigators. If it was up to me, I'd drive my car, but the department's insurance wouldn't cover any damage to my classic girl."

Girl? How could I not know? He already has a girlfriend in—

He leans toward me. "Are you okay? You look a little green around the gills."

Despite my half-elf, one-quarter angel, one-quarter human DNA, I'm certain I don't have gills. And I definitely don't want to put Keith on the spot by asking about his actual girlfriend.

As though Keith can read my mind, he leans back, laughs, and rubs his hands along the steering wheel before pulling into the street. "I see where I messed up. When I said *girl*, I meant my car. I've got a 1966 Charger that I rebuilt from the ground up. She's worth a fortune. I call her Fallen Angel, and I tend to be overly sentimental about that pile of old nuts and bolts." He chuckles as he makes the turn for the station.

My shoulders straighten, and it seems the weight of the world has been lifted. "Sounds beautiful. I've never heard anyone refer to a car that way. Maybe I can take a look at her?"

He agrees for a moment and then shakes his head. "I have the old girl packed away for winter. If I didn't have the luxury of this department issue car, I'd have no choice but to drive her in the winter. But, since I got these wheels, I keep her off the icy roads as much as possible. You never know when they're gonna dump salt or gravel on the roads. That would definitely damage her Sublime paint job."

I nod, as though I have some idea what he's talking about.

"Technically, that color wasn't available until 1970, but I wasn't doing a numbers-matching restoration."

"Hmmm." So, *Sublime* is a color. Keith is chock full of interesting facts.

The quaint brick sheriff's station pops into view as we head up the hill. Like many of the old buildings in town, the station has living quarters above.

"Does anyone live above the station?"

Keith glances at the structure. "Not since the mid-1900s. Now we use it for file and equipment storage. Why? You looking to move?"

"Move? Me? No—"

His warm laughter fills the car as he maneuvers into a parking spot. "I'm just joshin' with you, eh?"

"Oh, okay." Joshin' must be something like kidding. It seems humans are obsessed with humor.

We jump out of the vehicle, and I reach the door ahead of him, perhaps too eager for my spy mission.

"Slow down, Cindy. I need to assess the situation in there before I put you in the observation room. If Deputy Rivera is on shift, we might have to come up with a different plan."

"Got it. No problem."

He holds the door for me as we step inside. Deputy Chrisp rolls her chair back from her desk. Her boots squeak against the speckled linoleum as she walks toward us, past the row of dark, wooden built-in cabinets reaching almost to the ceiling. "Are you questioning Ms. Claus again?"

He shakes his head and lifts both hands. "No. No. Cindy and I have plans. She's just going to hang out while I conduct the interview. Who's on shift?"

Chrisp makes a grand gesture of looking over

both of her square shoulders, as well as putting a hand above her eyes to peer into the distance before replying. "You're lookin' at her."

Keith chuckles, thanks the deputy, and motions for me to follow him.

She returns to her desk as Keith opens the door to the observation room and ushers me inside. "I'll turn the speaker on, and you can hang out here. Who knows, you might pick up on something that I miss. It shouldn't take me long to get the information I need. Are you serious about cookies at your place?"

Hoping I'm getting the hang of human sarcasm, I paint my features into a stern expression. "Serious as a blizzard, Deputy."

His laughter echoes in the spartan room, and he slips out, closing the door behind him.

About three minutes later, a door opens into a room on the other side of a large window, and Keith places Bolton Oswald on the opposite side of the table, in a chair facing me, while he pulls out the second chair with its back to me.

My throat tightens and my tongue swells from dryness as Bolton seems to stare directly at me. Keith didn't mention anything about Mr. Oswald being able to see me! His gaze makes me so uncomfortable I have to get out of my chair and pace.

As I do so, Bolton's eyes don't follow me. Maybe he can't see me. Maybe it's like my magic globe back at the North Pole, where I can place my finger on any location in the world and see what's happening there, but the people at that location can't see me.

I'll test the theory.

Stepping closer to the window, I make a silly face and flap my arms like a puffin, and when my actions receive no response from Mr. Oswald, I'm satisfied that whatever magic this window holds, I can't be seen. A sigh of relief escapes as I return to the chair.

By the time I satisfy my curiosity and start paying attention, Keith is questioning Bolton about the crime that landed him in jail.

"Ron Schmenkel is the one that put you away for armed robbery and grand theft auto, correct?"

Bolton fidgets in his chair and looks down. "Yeah. I was away clean. Ditched the car, hopped on my sled, and ripped three miles into the backcountry. I holed up at a cabin owned by my ex-wife's uncle. That dang Schmenkel had to pick that weekend to go ice fishing. He saw smoke coming out of the chimney. Next thing I know, I'm looking at twenty-five years." Mr. Oswald pushes back from the metal table and exhales.

"How did you bypass the fingerprint ID alarm?"

Mr. Oswald straightens and presses his back into the chair. "I didn't. It was down for maintenance. That's why I hit the place."

"You're sure?" Keith's voice is cold as ice.

"Yeah. Yeah, I'm sure." Bolton shifts in his chair.

"The court transcripts indicate you made threats against Mr. Schmenkel at the sentencing hearing. Is that correct?"

Bolton scoffs. "Sounds to me like you got it all figured out, college boy. If you have the transcripts, why are you asking me?"

"I'd like to hear what happened in your own words, Mr. Oswald." Cool as an iceberg.

Mr. Oswald licks his lips and looks toward the side wall. "Yeah. I was upset. I said a bunch of stuff. Didn't mean it. Did my time. Mended my ways."

Keith leans back and quietly studies the man's actions. Bolton picks at invisible dirt in his cuticles and sniffs sharply every few seconds.

"I gotta say, Mr. Oswald. You seem nervous. That's not the behavior of a man who's mended his ways."

Bolton tips back, angling his gaze toward the

ceiling before furiously rubbing both hands over his face. "I been trying, all right. I grabbed some cash off the tables. I was a little short making my rent this month. I didn't think Zahara would mind."

Keith leans back in his chair and lets silence hang in the air. Mr. Oswald goes still as stone.

"Thank you for your cooperation, Mr. Oswald. I'll be releasing you. I suggest you return to D'lish and tell Zahara what you've done. She seems like the kind of woman who'd forgive that. I would also advise you not to leave town."

Bolton gets to his feet and a hint of anger returns to his features. "I'm still a suspect?"

"I'm afraid so, sir. Regardless of your claim that you've mended your ways, you did make threats against Ronnie Schmenkel's life, you had the cake pan from Yuletide Me Over Bakery, and you don't have an alibi for the time of his death."

Bolton exhales as his hands ball into fists. "'Course I don't have an alibi for last Wednesday between 10:00 a.m. and noon. I didn't do anything wrong. Didn't know I'd need one. Seems like it'd be worse if I had an alibi."

Keith leans toward the suspect and lowers his voice. "Like I said, you're free to leave the station. Just don't leave the city." He holds the door for Mr.

Oswald, and the ex-con turned dishwasher trudges out of the station.

Before leaving the room, Keith glances at the large window and offers a shrug.

Wait! Can he see me?

CHAPTER 14

*K*eith cracks open the door to the observation room. "My apologies. It took longer than I'd hoped. Let me get you home. I know you have to get an early start."

Ten different things are fighting for front and center in my head. "Can you see through that window?" ends up the winner.

"This window?" He points to the large square pane of glass. "Oh no. Not at all. I should've told you. It's one-way glass. There's a mirrored coating on the other side. So, you can see into the interrogation room, but the occupants can't see out."

"You looked at me and—"

"Well, sure. I knew you were in here. I just assumed you'd be looking. Don't worry. He had no idea you were in here."

"Thank goodness. Whew. Bolton made it clear he didn't like me when I ran into him at D'lish. I definitely don't want him to know I'm poking around in Ronnie's case."

Leading the way out of the station, Keith calls over his shoulder, "He won't hear it from me."

Energy buzzes through my limbs as we walk to the car. "How do you get any sleep?"

Keith opens the car door for me, and, once we're headed back toward our apartments, he replies, "What do you mean? Are you asking me if I have a guilty conscience?"

"Gosh. No. That's not what I meant. The investigating . . . It's so exciting."

He effortlessly parallel parks in front of our building and turns off the engine. "I'll admit, in the beginning it was difficult to unwind when I was in the middle of a big case. Now, I take my mental health seriously and have two or three different go-to methods for settling myself down for a good night's sleep." He pauses and gazes at me. "Sounds like you might be a bit too wound up for bedtime."

"I am. My brain is spinning! I just keep going over the evidence in my head and trying to figure out what could have happened."

"So, do you still have the energy for cookies?"

He pauses on the landing between our apartments and spins his keys around his finger.

"Oh, definitely. Come on in!" I unlock the door, and he follows me into the apartment. Artikoa leaps off the green velvet chair and places himself firmly in front of Keith.

"Hey, buddy, Cindy and I need to debrief about Ronnie's case. Is that okay with you?"

"Arti, you don't need to protect me from Keith." As I busy myself in the kitchen making hot chocolate, Artikoa relents. He returns to one of the armchairs, and Keith takes the other.

Serving up the hot chocolate, I add extra marshmallows and load a plate with Santa's Surprise Peanut Butter Cookies.

Keith eagerly grabs a cookie, and, through a mouthful, he utters his praise. "These are delicious. Another secret recipe?"

"Yes. These were the first cookies I learned how to make when I was working at the bakery in the North—"

"YIP."

My eyes meet Keith's, and the warmth projecting toward me removes my self-conscious worry.

He gestures to the chair Artikoa occupies. "How about you let Cindy have a seat, buddy? I'll bring you a nice bone from the butcher shop tomorrow."

Almost instantly, Artikoa leaps from the chair.

Keith chuckles. "If I didn't know better, I'd say that dog of yours speaks English."

Once again, my inner compulsion toward honesty overrides my instinct for self-preservation. "He does. And several other languages." Before Artikoa can offer a yip of correction, Keith laughs heartily.

Whew! One thing I'm learning about humans is how unlikely they are to believe things outside the realm of what they consider normal. In Keith's world, humans don't have arctic foxes as their companions. Furthermore, those foxes are not venerable elders who speak multiple languages. Nevertheless, I need to be more careful. I'm sure Artikoa will lecture me the moment Keith leaves.

"What did you think of the interrogation, Cindy?"

Dunking my cookie into my hot chocolate, I savor the result as I replay the sentence. "I have pretty good instincts about people." I'll spare him the lecture on my Nice and Naughty List insights. "And even though Bolton tends to think of himself first in every situation, I didn't get the feeling he was lying. I really don't think he had anything to do with Ronnie's death. Oh, and also, I believe he found that pan on the sidewalk."

"I hate to say, but so do I. The question remains, who dropped it there? Whoever discarded that pan, has to be the person who planted your prints at the scene."

Shrugging my shoulders, I can't think of a single plausible explanation.

Keith and I continue to mull over the details of the interview and, in the end, he mostly agrees with me.

"I better let you get some sleep. I'll stop by the bakery in the morning for coffee and an apple dumpling — in Ronnie's honor."

"You got it." A half-hearted grin hovers. I'd secretly love for him to stay longer, but there's no way I'm mentioning that in front of a judgey fox.

He offers Artikoa a rough pat on the head and takes his leave.

Waiting to hear Keith's door locking behind him, I turn to take my lecture like a grown elf. Instead, I face an oddly gentle fox. "Perhaps my judgment of humans has been too hasty. This particular creature seems trustworthy."

"Of course he is. You worry too much."

Artikoa scoffs and curls up on the green velvet armchair. "Is that pan on the counter an item of some importance?"

As I pull back my covers, I give Arti a heavily abbreviated version of the night's events.

"You'll need to rise on the bright, Cynthia. I'll take a quick sniff around the back room before you open. Perhaps I can uncover the scent of an intruder."

"'Kay." Collapsing into bed in my Krampus sweater, my dreams are filled with dark creatures lurking in the shadows and children running from glittering bundles of birch twigs.

Morning comes far too soon, and I find myself scurrying around the apartment in a way that reminds me distinctly of being late to my shift at the factory in the North Pole.

"Your search of the bakery will have to wait, Arti. I'm late!"

Unable to find my favorite sweater — the one with my father's face embroidered on the front — I'm forced to wear the Krampus shirt one more day. When I enter the bakery, Jasmine glances at the time on her phone, takes one look at my sweater, and chuckles wickedly. "Same clothes as yesterday, and you're running late? Is this a walk of shame situation?"

Apparently, my emotions are easier to read than I'd imagined. I'm ashamed to be wearing the same sweater. "I couldn't find my favorite sweater. It's just—"

"JK, Cindy." She laughs outright and hands me a cup of coffee. "Keith hardly seems like a lowlife dude who'd try something on a first date."

As though the mere mention of his name could summon him, Keith saunters into the bakery. "Morning, Jasmine. Can you heat me up an apple dumpling?"

"Totes." She turns to me and flashes her eyebrows as she fulfills Keith's order.

He takes one look at my bleary eyes and large mug of coffee, and grins. "Did you get any sleep?"

"A bit. I had weird dreams."

"Sorry to hear that." His concern is genuine.

"Here or to-go, Mr. Winters?"

He looks at his watch and blows a raspberry. "Yup. Better make it to-go."

Jasmine packages up his dumpling, puts a lid on his coffee cup, and accepts the cash in exchange.

"Take it easy, Mr. Winters."

Keith nods politely. "Will do." He pauses. "Hey, you don't know anything about a pan ending up on the sidewalk, do you, Jasmine?"

Her big blue eyes dart toward me and quickly back to Keith. "Is this about that missing pan?"

We both nod.

"So, like —" Jasmine fiddles with her phone

and her gaze tracks everywhere except on Keith or me. "I should've fessed when you asked me. I kinda left the counter for a few the other day."

My mouth opens, but it's Keith who poses the question. "You left the bakery unattended? Did you lock the door?"

"Not exactly." She tucks her phone into the pocket of her red apron. "I had to go — use the — you know." Jasmine waves one hand absently toward the restroom. "There were, like, three ladies in here. I told 'em I'd be right back."

Sounds innocent enough to me. "That's okay, Jazz. I'm sorry I wasn't here to step in for you."

She bites her lip and nods quickly.

Keith isn't done. "Were all three ladies here when you came back?"

"I think— Hold up." Jasmine looks at the tables and points her fingers as her gaze seems to replay a memory. "The two ladies with hella shopping bags were here, but the solo flyer with the bougie tote was gone."

"Do you remember anything about her besides the fancy bag?" Keith steps closer and leans in.

"Nah. Sorry, guys." Her gaze drops to the floor.

Placing a hand on her shoulder, I offer what I can. "Don't worry about it. We got the pan back. So, no problem. Okay?"

Jasmine looks at me from the corner of her eye. "You're not gonna fire me?"

"Of course not!" Patting her back, I wish I could think of more to say, but my experience as a boss is quite limited.

"I better get to the station. If that woman with the nice tote bag comes in, call me."

"Okay." I wish he had time to sit down over coffee. "Bye, Keith."

"I'll catch up with you later, Cindy."

He waves and exits.

As I reach for my green apron, I'm overcome with the urge to go to the laundromat and see if I somehow left my sweater in one of the dryers. It has to be somewhere. I turned my apartment inside out, and that place is simply not big enough to lose anything in.

Turning to Jasmine, I announce my plans.

"No prob. I can hold down the fort for a bit."

"Thanks."

Taking the stairs two at a time, I burst into the apartment and grab my coat.

"And where are you suddenly headed?" Artikoa's ears perk to attention, and he appears ready to leap.

"I think I left my favorite sweater at the laundromat. It's gotta be in one of those dryers."

"I'll accompany you. I could do with a morning constitutional."

Rolling my eyes as I button my coat, I make no verbal protest.

The wily fox races ahead of me as I march toward the laundromat.

Todd Freeman is shoveling some wind-blown snowdrifts from the sidewalk when I approach.

"I wondered how long it would take?"

Mr. Freeman has always been a curmudgeon, but unless I'm terribly mistaken, there's a hint of warmth underlying his crotchety tone. "How long it would take for what?"

He leans his shovel against the building and motions for me to follow him inside.

Stepping into a tiny office in the back corner of the laundromat, he returns with a carefully folded bundle.

"My sweater!"

An unusually hospitable look erupts on Todd's face. "I was pretty sure you didn't leave it here on purpose." He passes me the bundle, and I hug it tightly to my chest. "Never. This is my absolute favorite. Papa gave it to me for my 100th—" If Artikoa were allowed inside, he would certainly be yipping. At least this time, I stopped myself.

"Anyway, how are you and that deputy doing on Ronnie's case?"

The small-town rumor mill has simultaneously cleared me of blame and put me on the side of the law. "Seems like we've reached another dead end. We had a decent suspect, but I don't think that's gonna lead anywhere. Just have to look at the evidence again."

"Have you talked to that Myra woman?"

"Myra? Do you mean Mona, Sven's wife?"

He scoffs. "If I meant Mona, I'd say Mona. I mean Myra Patara. She's that property developer who was trying to buy the building from Ronnie. Pushy broad."

"Ronnie was selling the building?" This was news to me. Why would he announce he was going to leave it to me if—

Todd shakes his head vigorously. "No siree. Ronnie flat-out refused that woman time after time. She had some plans to bulldoze everything and put in something she called a 'boutique hotel.' Ronnie wasn't having none of it."

Hugging the sweater tightly, I step toward the door. "Thanks, Todd. For the sweater and the lead. I'll let Keith know right away."

As I walk out of the laundromat, Todd's chuckle echoes off the linoleum. "Oh, it's Keith now, is it?"

Seems like he'll have a new bit of grist for the rumor mill.

CHAPTER 15

*E*lven instincts take over as I practically fly up the hill toward my bakery. Artikoa is left in my wake. Lucky for me, the only witnesses to my inhuman speed are a few parked cars and an abandoned grocery cart.

If only I had one of those mobile telephones. I don't really have anyone to call, but it seems like it would be a handy item to have in urgent circumstances.

As I burst into the bakery like a winter storm, all heads turn. The first thing that pops into my head flops from my mouth. Waving the bundle in the air, I shout, "I found it!"

Jasmine's uproarious laughter forces her to lean on the counter for support as she guffaws.

Taking a cue from her, several of my clients chuckle along.

My cheeks emanate a rosy glow as I shake my head and run upstairs.

Changing into my favorite sweater, I don a lovely pair of red leggings dotted with green Christmas trees. Before I return to the bakery, ready to face the day, I have to let Keith know what I heard at the laundromat.

Grabbing the receiver from the cradle, I place the call. "Keith! You'll never guess what I just found out."

There's a pause, and then he makes it clear he doesn't know and I should go ahead and tell him.

"Of course. I was going to tell you. I just — never mind. I found my sweater at the laundromat."

A brief chuckle travels down the phone line, and he asks if he should alert the media.

"Gosh, golly. I'm messing this up. What I meant to tell you is the news that came from Mr. Freeman. He told me there's some real estate developer in town, Myra Patara, who was trying to buy Ronnie's building and set up a thing called a 'boutique hotel.'"

Keith reminds me that Ronnie had promised the building to me.

"I know. But Todd said Ronnie wasn't going to

sell it to this lady. He said the woman just kept making offers, and Ronnie kept turning her down. That could be something, right?"

Keith agrees and promises to track down Myra Patara and bring her in for questioning.

Returning to the bakery, I lose myself in the dough. Proving, rolling, and more proving. I've always loved making bread.

Once the cinnamon rolls and the sourdough are set for their final proof, it's time to take my lunch break. When my eyes catch sight of the clock, I can hardly believe it's nearly 1:00 p.m.

As I emerge from the back room, Jazz has a strange smirk on her face. She arches one eyebrow and looks toward the door.

Glancing in the indicated direction, a ready smile lifts my cheeks when I catch sight of Keith stomping the snow off his boots in the entryway.

"Hey, Cindy. Any chance you can take a break?"

"Of course. What can I get you?"

He takes three long strides toward me and lowers his voice. "I have some leftover beef stroganoff in my apartment. If you don't mind eating lefties, I'd like to discuss the case without setting off any alarm bells in the local gossip group."

His nearness sends a flush of warmth down my arms. "I don't generally eat meat."

"Oh, right. How about tomato soup and grilled cheese?"

"That's perfect." Turning to Jasmine, I plan to negotiate, but she's a step ahead. "Chill and take your lunch, boss. I'll snack on a carrot cookie and bust outta here when you get back." She lifts her right hand, palm facing me. "I swear I won't leave the counter unattended."

"Thank you!" After hanging my green apron on the hook, I follow Keith up to his apartment.

Artikoa vanished after I left him in my snow wake on the way home from the laundromat, so there's no one to scold me when I step into Keith's apartment unescorted.

His living space is utilitarian — the complete opposite of the former occupant. Betty was all color and clutter. Keith's décor consists of a plain brown couch, a compact square dining table with two chairs, an ancient coffee table with two deep scratches in the surface, and a large TV on a rickety black shelving unit. The only item that doesn't blend into the background is a handmade broom mounted on the wall above the sofa.

The handle is birch, still sporting the distinct black and white bark, and one broomcorn looks as though it's been dipped in gold. What an odd piece.

Keith has been busy in the kitchen. The delicious aroma of toasting sandwiches and bubbling soup fills his humble abode and distracts me from my musings.

Sitting at the whitewashed dining table, in the only two chairs he owns, we hungrily tuck into lunch. "Mmmm. This grilled cheese is amazing. How do you get the outside so crispy?"

"I learned the trick from my grandmother before she passed. Instead of buttering the outside of the bread, she would use mayonnaise. Somehow, that made the sandwich toast up extra crispy and makes it taste better altogether — in my opinion."

"I agree. And I'm sorry for your loss." Now that I've lost Ronnie, I have a deeper understanding of what it means for these humans to lose their loved ones.

Keith inhales slowly and leans back in his chair. "Thank you. My grandma was an amazing woman. There was always room at her table. She never shied away from a hug. Honestly, you remind me of her."

Judging by the emotions on his face, this seems like a compliment. "Thank you. I wish I could've met her."

"Me too. Losing her definitely left a hole in my life. My parents were great, but there's just something about a grandma's love that can't be duplicated."

Never having had a grandmother, I have no idea what Keith is describing. However, even without a yip from Artikoa, I know this is something that should not be discussed. Better to shift the conversation to the case.

"Did you get a chance to question Myra?"

"I've got the deputies tracking her down. Hopefully, they'll bring her in this afternoon. Meanwhile, we received the fingerprint results, taken off that rolling pin stand, from AFIS. No matches. I was really hoping something would come up." His chin drops, and he lays his spoon on the table. "Felt certain the print from the rolling pin base would tie to one of the criminals Ronnie put away. Anybody that he'd processed would've had prints on file. Looks like we've got a brilliant piece of evidence that absolutely takes us nowhere. Not exactly sure what to do next."

"Shoot! I don't know what an aphis is, but that definitely is disappointing."

He gazes at me with wide-eyed wonder, and his eyes linger on my face. "Acronyms become a force of habit in my line of work. AFIS is a national fingerprint database. Technically, it's a biometric identification system that uses digital imaging technology to evaluate fingerprint data. There are millions of prints on file. It's not foolproof. A lot of older information is missing, and there are certainly some small jurisdictions that don't have the manpower to participate, but it was definitely our best hope and it was a flat-out dead end."

A disappointed silence hangs between us as we finish our lunch.

"Maybe they'll find out where Myra is staying, and you can talk to her this afternoon. I bet she can tell you more about this boutique hotel business."

Keith clears my dishes away and refills my water. "Hey, were you serious about helping out with the funeral? When I notified his kids, they made it clear they wouldn't be coming to town. Made a bunch of weak excuses about finances and babysitters. Real shame."

I certainly can't back out now. "That's awful. Ronnie was always so kind to me. I'd be honored to help. Did you get hold of the will?"

"Unofficially. The official reading of the will is supposed to be the day before the funeral, per Mr. Schmenkel's instructions. I was able to convince the lawyer that there wouldn't be a funeral if we weren't made aware of Mr. Schmenkel's preferences. He agreed to release that part of Ronnie's last will and testament to the department. So if you're serious about helping, I'll give you a copy of the page that mentions the memorial service."

"Okay. Sure. I'll get started right away."

Keith walks over to a tattered leather satchel, flips it open, and digs through some files. "Here it is." He returns to the table and hands me a sheet of paper. "I've got another copy, so you can keep this one."

"Thanks." Gazing at the type-written lines, my mind goes to an image of Ronnie discussing these arrangements with Connie when she was alive. It's not a vision or anything magical, just something I can imagine.

"Is Eastwell's Funeral Home something local?"

"Yup. Family-run business for almost a century, from what I hear. They buried everybody in town for as long as there's been a town. Although, with the ground frozen solid, as it is this time of year, they won't be able to bury Ronnie until the spring thaw."

Too many questions are flooding my brain. I'll simply give myself a chance to read everything over and save my questions for the funeral home.

"Thanks for letting me do this, Keith. Ronnie was my first friend in Silver Shoals. I feel a connection to him, and even to Connie. Feels good to be useful."

Deep sadness flashes across Keith's face, and he swallows with difficulty. "It's not easy, but it helps."

He must be thinking of his grandmother.

Strange how, even with their short lifespans, humans can make such lasting impacts on one another.

After thanking Keith for lunch, I place the important paper in my apartment before returning to the bakery.

Traffic is lighter than normal at the bakery, and I leave Jasmine to close up while I place a quick call to the funeral home that secures me an appointment a mere thirty minutes from now.

"Jazz, I need to head over to— I have an appointment. You okay to close up on your own?"

"Sure enough." She offers me a thumbs up, and I head out the door.

The sun is high in the sky. The lack of cloud cover has produced a sharp drop in temperature.

With my precious sheet of Ronnie's instructions in hand, I head down to the funeral home located two blocks past the hardware store. Frida is cleaning the inside of the huge front windows when I walk by, and she offers a friendly wave through the glass. I return her greeting.

The kind gesture brings a swell of unbidden emotions. Picking up my pace, I blink back tears and hurry toward Eastwell's.

The building is impossible to miss. A brick structure, with what appears to be a church attached. There are stained-glass windows depicting peaceful garden scenes on either side of double wooden doors. A brass plaque with black letters indicates "Office" to the right.

I open the single glass door, and the suffocating silence envelops me. There's an odd, musty odor paired with something else I can't identify. Some ancient antiseptic. The lighting is dim overhead, but individual spotlights illuminate several hand-painted portraits of various Eastwells adorning the wall.

A thick wooden door creaks open to my left and startles me.

"Good afternoon. How may we ease your journey?"

An icy chill tightens the skin on my face. "I'm Cindy. I have an appointment."

The gentle, sonorous voice of the man in front of me continues, "Cindy, I am Victor Eastwell. Please follow me."

He tugs the hem of his wrinkled navy-blue suit jacket and leads me to an office. Three beige walls are bare, but the wall behind him contains myriad framed certificates. My eyes scan the type. Words like mortician, state license, and cremation twist at my insides.

"I understand you've been chosen to facilitate the last wishes of Mr. Schmenkel. Is that correct?"

"Yes. His lawyer— I have—" Words are

trapped in my constricted throat. I shove the single sheet of paper in front of Mr. Eastwell.

His practiced eyes flow over the page with ease. "Very standard. How soon would you like to have the service?"

"I think we'd like to have it before Christmas."

Mr. Eastwell's pale eyes flood with deep understanding. "Yes, it would be comforting for the family to have closure before the holidays. When do his children arrive?"

His children! What can I tell him about Ronnie's children? I have no idea how to explain why they refused to come to his funeral. Can I side-step the truth? "I'll have to ask Mr. Winters." That'll do for now.

"Of course. I'll schedule the service for December 23rd. Shall we post the obituary? Will there be a dress code or preference? Do you have a preference for flowers?"

"Flowers? At the funeral?" My lack of practical human knowledge is flooding me with a suffocating lack of confidence.

"At the memorial service. As you know, we cannot permanently lay Mr. Schmenkel to rest until the spring thaw." His thin lips attempt to curl upward, but I sense frustration setting in. "Let's put a pin in the flowers and select the casket." Mr.

Eastwell rises in one smooth motion. "Follow me, dear."

On second thought, this is entirely too much humanity for one day. I admire these mortal creatures, and their internal strength, but I can't muster any. "What is— Why—?"

Victor places a pale white hand on my arm. "I know this is difficult, Cindy."

One sheet of paper. One simple list of instructions. I'm utterly overcome. If this is what it is like to deal with death and its aftermath, I want nothing to do with it.

"I'll leave it up to you. That paper I gave you. You've read his—"

"Don't give it a second thought, dear. The information you've provided is more than sufficient. Leave it with me." He extends his hand. "We'll welcome you and yours on the 23rd."

Blindly shaking Mr. Eastwell's hand, I flee from the mortuary and rush up the hill to the comforting safety of my apartment.

CHAPTER 16

*a*s I stand in an unfamiliar room, a monstrous presence seems to lurk in the shadows. The room begins to spin—

Gentle knocking at my door pulls me from the terrible dream.

Did I imagine . . .

A lone tear trickles down my cheek. As I hurry to the kitchen to dry my face, another knock startles me. "Who is it?"

"It's Keith. You all right in there?"

After a steadying breath, I reply, "Yeah. Just a bad dream." When I open the door, Keith takes one look at me and tilts his head. "You look like you could use a hug."

The last word has scarcely formed before I

throw my arms around his neck and press my cheek against his soft blue sweater.

"Hey, hey. That must've been some nightmare. You sure you're okay?"

"The whole funeral thing. It was—" Too conscious of his nearness, I lean away and swipe a hand under each eye. "It was a lot."

"Did you go to Eastwell's today?"

"Yes. I didn't do much." Sharp inhale. "I left the instructions with Mr. Eastwell."

"Oh, I thought— Surely you've been to a funer—" He stops mid-sentence and regroups. "That must've been hard for you."

All I can do is shake my head and blink back tears.

"Did you— Were you able to—" Keith clearly doesn't want to finish the sentence, nor do I want him to.

"Mr. Eastwell mentioned Ronnie's family. I didn't know what to tell him."

"I'll give Eastwell's a call and give him a sanitized version of the truth. I have to say, the kids were pretty unemotional. Seems like they had one heckuva dysfunctional relationship with Ronnie."

Chewing my bottom lip for a few seconds, I wonder if I've done the right thing. I better tell Keith. He'll know what to do. "The memorial service is going to be on the 23rd at 1:00 p.m. Should I call Ronnie's children?"

"I wouldn't ask you to do that. Not after what you went through earlier today. I'll give them both a call and give them a chance to change their minds about attending. You did a good thing for Ronnie. I wish it hadn't been so difficult for you." Keith slips an arm around my shoulders and gives me a kind squeeze. "I've got a bunch of paperwork to do — working late. Plus, the lawyer wants to schedule the reading of the will." He steps toward the stairs and looks back. "I probably won't see you until tomorrow. Take it easy on yourself, okay?"

"Okay." A ragged breath escapes, and I force myself to act brave as he descends.

At the bottom of the first flight, he looks back. "Maybe make yourself some hot chocolate. Wish I had time to enjoy it with you."

His positive energy boosts my morale. "Thanks. That's a great idea." He wishes he could hang out with me? Oh boy! That's better than any hot beverage.

MORNING BREAKS LIKE THE ARCTIC WIND against the magic bubble protecting the North Pole. I can't shake the feeling of a shadow from my dark dreams lingering on the fringes of the waking world. I don't dare tell Artikoa. He'll tattle on me, and that's the last thing I need. I have to learn to take care of myself in this human world.

As I prepare to leave the apartment, I step on a piece of paper that was slipped under my door. Stooping to pick it up brings Artikoa out of nowhere to sit by my side. "What do you have there? Anything official?"

Chuckling, I glance down. "It's not from the North Pole, if that's what you mean." Fanning the paper toward the snoopy fox, I continue, "This is a note from Keith.

"'Dear Cindy, I spoke to Ronnie's son and daughter and they still claim they can't afford to make the trip. Can't take time off work. Can't find anyone to watch the kids. Same series of hollow excuses. Disappointing. The lawyer mentioned reading of the will was scheduled for today at 10:00 a.m. You're welcome to attend, although I'm certain Ronnie didn't have time to change the will before he passed away. I notified his children and Sven. I don't expect anyone but Sven to be there unless the lawyer has invited someone. I hope you got some nightmare-free sleep. All the best, Keith.'"

Artikoa's fluffy tail swishes twice. "It is a sad day indeed to have your children fail to attend your funeral." He clears his throat.

His words weigh heavily on my chest. "I agree."

"You've had unpleasant dreams?" Amber eyes study me closely.

"I don't know. It was weird. In the dream, I felt a dark energy. I couldn't imagine—"

The venerable elder leaps instantly onto all fours. His ears point in high alert. "Was it a premonition?"

"No, nothing like that. I'm sure of it. Just an awful nightmare. It made me worry about Papa, and wonder if I messed up by leaving home."

Artikoa hesitates, then brushes against my leg. "You're a good daughter, Cynthia. You may not have chosen to follow in your father's footsteps, but he knows how much you love him."

This unusual display of affection from the most venerable elder pushes the pent-up tears from my eyes in a torrent.

Collapsing to the floor, I scoop my arms around him and let my tears soak into the soft fur.

To his credit, he does not pull away — at first.

After two or three minutes of my emotional outburst, he wriggles free and wipes his wet fur against the quilt on my bed. "You must pull yourself together and get down to the bakery, Cynthia."

"Right." Placing Keith's note on the kitchen table, I dry my eyes, twist my wild red hair up into a messy bun, and inhale deeply. I definitely won't be attending the reading of the will. I'm not family, and my presence would only make Sven uncomfortable.

The best thing to do is throw myself into my work.

Morning at the bakery proves a worthy distraction. At one point, the order line almost reaches back to the entrance. Jasmine's hands fly in and out of the case and over the knobs and levers on the espresso machine with confidence. My plan to lose myself in baking will have to wait. There are just too many customers up front.

Eventually, the crowd thins, and I encourage Jasmine to take her break first.

"Thanks, boss. I need it."

Wiping her hands on her red apron, she whips up an enormous cup of coffee for herself, and I place three carrot cookies on a plate.

She greedily takes the plate. "Yikes! You know my weakness."

No sooner does she disappear into the back room with her tray of treats than the towering form of Sven Tollesson enters my bakery.

There are bags under his eyes, and it's clear he's been getting about as much sleep as me. Although, there's a lightness to his step that I haven't seen since Ronnie's death.

"Mornin', Cindy. Not sure if you knew or not, but they read Ronnie's will today."

"Mr. Winters mentioned it to me. How did it go?"

Emotion temporarily pinches his features, and he draws a ragged breath. "I wish his kids would've been there. Left each of 'em a bit of money and some stuff for the grandkids. Shame they couldn't make the trip."

Offering silent agreement with a simple tilt of my head, I attempt to stick to the facts. "It is. Mr. Winters said they couldn't afford—"

One huge paw waves away my objection. "Pshaw! Those kids never forgave their dad for spending their inheritance on Connie's bakery. Never was their money. Gotta make your own way in this world."

Strange that he would say that when he seemed so eager to get his hands on this building. Probably best to keep that thought to myself. "What about the building?"

Sven nods and shoves his hands into his pockets. "I wish I hadn't had such harsh words with Ronnie. Terrible thing to have weighing on my conscience."

He didn't answer my question, but it's best to let him get there in his own time.

"He did leave the building to me and Mona,

and he left us his house as well."

"Will you be moving into his house?" My mind swirls, and I shove away the images of Ronnie lying on that green shag carpet in his living room. Odd name for the place where he ceased to be alive . . .

Sven shakes his head and strokes his thick beard. "No. No. The missus and I talked about it. It's just too small. We'll have to sell it, and then we can use that money to help take care of the family. I'm sure Ronnie would've wanted that."

Having no idea what Ronnie would or wouldn't have wanted, I dip my chin in agreement and remain silent.

"Now that you're my landlord, would it be considered a bribe if I gave you half a dozen cinnamon rolls to take home?"

For a moment, the old Sven is visible behind the thick beard and the mask of grief. "That sounds wonderful! But, truth is, I'm not the one who'll be your new landlord."

"What? I thought you said Ronnie left you the building?"

"Oh, for sure. For sure. The strangest thing happened on the way home from the lawyer's office. I got a call from a woman named Myra Patara. She met me down at the sign shop and offered me a price on this building I couldn't refuse." He squares his shoulders proudly. "So not much will change for you. And I'm sure she'll introduce herself when the time is right."

"You sold the building to Myra Patara?"

Sven beams with pride and lifts his work pail in my direction like a toast. "Sure did. And I came up here to paint that sign on the new window over there in your overflow seating area. In fact, I'm feeling so good about things today, I'm gonna give you fifty percent off."

A muffled thanks is all I can manage.

"You want me to paint it in the same Christmas Cheer font? Letters in Santa's Sleigh red with the filigree outline?"

Sven's kind offer temporarily throws me off kilter. "Sure. I love the original window lettering you painted for me. So that'd be great."

"You betcha." He bends toward me. "And if you can make that eight cinnamon rolls, I sure would appreciate it. Gotta have one for each of the hungry mouths at home, plus one for me and one for the missus."

A girl with flaxen hair and bright-blue eyes peeks out from behind the behemoth of a man. At six-feet tall, she's still head and shoulders below her dad. "Would it be all right with you if I do some of the painting, Cindy?"

"You must be Linnéa? I'd love it if you did

some of the painting. I saw your work in your father's shop and I was so impressed."

The humble fourteen-year-old lowers her eyelids and kicks the toe of her shoe against the floor. "Thanks. I've been practicing since I was, like, five, you know?"

"Well, I know your dad's awful proud."

"Thanks." She takes the pail of supplies from her father and turns to head into the overflow seating area.

As soon as she's out of earshot, I step towards Sven. "Sven, I'm really glad you found a buyer for the building, but I have some bad news."

His tawny-brown eyes widen, and he leans down to hear me better. "Something about Ronnie and, you know, the murder?"

"No. I heard that Myra Patara plans to bulldoze this entire building and put in some kind of swanky hotel. She's a developer from one of the big cities down south. I don't think she has any interest in being a landlord."

Sven reels backward as though struck by an invisible blow. "Are you pullin' my leg?"

Glancing down at his enormous limbs, I shake my head. "No. I'm not touching your legs."

He shakes his head and waves away my confusion. "Just an expression. Well, I gotta track down that Mrs. Patara and tell her a thing or two. I bet Ronnie's lawyer can get me out of that contract."

For a split second, I'm concerned he's leaving Linnéa unsupervised, but my larger concern is losing my entire livelihood if Myra Patara gets her hands on this building. So I cross my arms over my chest and let Sven continue his hunt.

I'd hate to be Mrs. Patara.

Calling after him, I attempt to offer something positive. "I'll send the cinnamon rolls with Linnéa."

One enormous arm waves in acknowledgment, but the angry bear does not pause.

I better head into the back and package up those rolls. I don't want to land on Sven's Naughty List!

CHAPTER 17

*N*ot more than thirty minutes later, a furious woman storms into the coffee shop, shouting my name. "Cindy? Cindy Claus?"

From the safety of the back room, I can't see what's happening, but Jasmine must offer her a cup of coffee. There's a pause in the rant, and the customers all return to their snacks and gossip.

However, three minutes later—

"Is that her? Is she in the back?"

And then a woman topped with raven-black hair jutting at wild angles from her scalp, and shoulders nearly as broad as Sven's, bursts into the back room, causing me to spill a bowl of icing for the batch of carrot cookies I'm making. "You're not allowed— You can't be—"

"Aha! I knew I'd find you here. Are you the one who manipulated Mr. Tollesson into questioning our contract?"

This must be the infamous Myra Patara.

"I didn't manipulate anyone. I told him the truth. Which is apparently something you avoided."

Her eyes crackle with what seems to be actual fire, and she steps closer. "I would have been satisfied with destroying your business. But your interference — an ancestral habit, by the way — forces me to do worse, Ms. Claus." Her entire face contorts as though the taste of my name on her tongue is rotten reindeer milk.

Deep inside me, possibly in the angel part of me, alarm bells sound. There's something distinctly unnatural about my unwelcome guest.

"I think you should leave, Mrs. Patara. I should warn you, I will be notifying the authorities of the threats you've made against me." I feel a burning need to detain her, but that's not my place, and I don't want to upset her any further. Keith and the deputies need to find her and talk to her. The best thing I can do is call Keith and let him know her whereabouts.

"Pathetic. Do you actually think these *people* scare me?"

Fire once again flickers in her eyes. She turns on her sharp-heeled shoes and clomps out of the bakery.

Jasmine pokes her head around the corner, opens her mouth in shock, and shakes her head. "That woman is salty as heck! I can't believe you kept your cool with her, boss. Impressive."

Now that the threat has been removed, a quiver of fear shakes my body. "Wow. She really was awful. I need to call Keith and let him know she paid me a visit."

"She left?"

Jasmine's question confuses me. Myra walked right past the counter. "Yeah, didn't you see her walk out?"

"Well, yeah. Totes. But, like, she left her coffee on the counter. I thought she was coming back."

Following Jasmine into the main room, I glance at the half-full mug on the countertop. "She was drinking from that?"

"For sure. Then she saw you in the back and just raged out."

"Jazz, do not touch that mug. Don't let anyone touch it."

She shrugs. "Whatevs. You're the boss."

Grabbing the receiver from the cradle, I dial Keith.

"Have the deputies had any luck tracking down Myra Patara?"

"No. She was supposedly staying at the Silver Shoals Inn, but we followed up with the owner, and Mrs. Patara had checked out this morning. Why?"

I give him the full report on my visit with Myra Patara, plus the fact that she walked out of my bakery not more than a minute before I called him.

There's a long, low whistle on the other end of the line. "You are something else, Cindy. Thanks for the hot tip."

I open my mouth to mention the mug, but he's too excited about his hot lead. He thanks me and says he's hopping in a cruiser with Deputy Chrisp to track down Mrs. Patara right now.

Before I can add a word, the line goes dead.

Shoot. I can't take a chance on losing potential evidence. I carefully slip Mrs. Patara's mug into a plastic bag, to keep it safe on a shelf until I can hand it off to Keith.

All this investigating has brought my appetite back.

"Jazz, can you put an apple dumpling on a plate for me?"

"Abso-frickin-lutely." She fills my order while I

step into the back room to clean up the icing mess before taking the dumpling up to my apartment to eat in peace.

"Cookie crumbs!" I hate wasting food, but there's no way I can save the icing. I'll have to make a new batch. Plus, I need to work fast so the now-cooled carrot cookies won't dry out.

Good thing I love my job!

LATER IN MY APARTMENT, I recount the afternoon's events to a surprisingly interested Artikoa. I have so garnered his attention that he leaves his bowl of raw chicken and steps closer to listen intently.

"And you're certain you sensed something, as you put it, unnatural, about this woman?" His white ears pinch together.

"Definitely. I've never felt it from any other human I've met."

His ears wilt. "You've hardly met more than a handful of humans, my dear. However, I admit this bears investigating."

"By me? You want me to follow her or something?"

All-knowing amber eyes lock onto me. "Not in the least. I will handle all reconnaissance. You will remain at the bakery, safe and sound. Do I have your word?"

My thoughts immediately jump to possible scenarios. "What if I need supplies for baking? Or if I need to do laundry?"

"I am quite certain this reconnaissance will take no more than a day. Once I have enough information to know exactly what we're dealing with, we will revisit your sequestering."

"Fine. I'll give you *one* day, but that's it. I can't be locked in this building forever. The whole reason I left the North Pole was to get some freedom." A dramatic exhale on my part brings the conversation to a sharp point.

"Cynthia Cherubim Claus, you're old enough to understand my intent is to preserve your safety, not to keep you prisoner."

"Fine."

Sulking above my apple dumpling, a knock on my door gives me such a start I drop my fork.

"Cindy? Are you in there? It's Keith."

Popping up from the chair, I jostle the table and send my glass of water tumbling.

The clatter brings Keith bursting through the door. "Sorry to barge in. I heard the crash."

Embarrassment colors my face as red as Santa's sleigh.

I carefully pick up the larger pieces of glass as

Keith heads for the kitchen. "I'll grab a towel to get the water. Be careful with the glass. Do you have a broom and dustpan?"

Tears spill from my eyes as I choke on my answer.

Keith drops to his knees beside me and removes the pieces of glass from my hand. "Hey, it's just a glass. I'm sure you have more, and, if you don't, I know a great antique store just down the road. There's no need to cry, Cindy." The thumb of his free hand wipes tears from my cheek.

"It's not the glass. It's Ronnie. I miss him. It's stupid. I barely knew the man. Don't know why I'm getting so emotional." I draw a skittering breath. "He was nice to me, you know?"

He finds the broom and dustpan, sweeps up the broken glass, and wipes up the water. Keith gives me space. He doesn't judge. All the while, he nods his head, affirming my emotional outburst.

"Is it always like this? Is it always so hard when someone dies?"

Keith dumps the last of the glass in the trash bin and tosses my dishtowel in the laundry basket in the corner. "Before I answer that, be careful with that dishtowel. There're all kinds of tiny shards of glass in there. Maybe you'll want to shake it out before you wash it. Just a reminder."

I nod and snuffle.

"Now, about your question. Every death is different. My mom told me that if you love someone when they're alive, you still feel that way about them after they're gone. Seems so simple, but I suppose people don't really think about it until it's too late. Ronnie was a good friend to you. Like you said, one of the first people you met in town. You two had a special bond because of the bakery and Connie's recipe books. It's perfectly normal that you would miss him and feel upset. Especially because he was taken from you — you know — too soon."

"Yeah, that makes sense. You must've loved your grandmother quite a bit."

The pain of loss gathers in Keith's eyes as he pulls me to my feet. "I did. She was the one person in my life who accepted me unconditionally. She didn't think it was weird that I was fascinated by the mystery of death when I wanted to know why this fish died, or why that squirrel died, or what kills humans. She even helped me research my options when I asked if there was a job where you could get paid to figure that out. Nana Winters loved me exactly as I was." He exhales and his eyes lose focus. "That was pretty hard to let go of."

Keith glances over my shoulder at the half-eaten dumpling. "May I sit down while you finish eating. and I'll tell you what we found out from Myra Patara?"

"You got her?"

"We did."

He pulls my chair back from the table, and I drop into it with a puzzled but pleased expression.

"It was a good thing you called the station when you did. Myra was gassing up her Apocalypse Hellfire 6 x 6—"

"She was driving a vehicle from Hell?" My mouth hangs open in horror.

"What?" Keith pulls his head back and scrunches up his face. "Oh, right. Sorry about that. I forget not everyone is into cars." He takes a breath and starts again. "She was putting fuel in her vehicle when we found her, and I guarantee you her next move was going to be to disappear. Deputy Rivera picked her up and brought her down to the station. Technically, she's not under arrest, but the fact that she attempted to flee points to a guilty conscience."

The good news fuels my appetite, and I take two bites of yum before responding. "Hooray. Don't keep me in suspense. What did you find out?"

His shoulders sag. "Not a gosh darn nothing."

"What? I thought you said Deputy Rivera brought her in?"

Keith places both of his elbows on the table and rests his chin in his hands. "Oh, he brought her in all right. The second he finished informing her of her Miranda rights, she asked for her attorney. No interview. No questions. No information."

"Stacks of snowballs!"

"Exactly. Without a stitch of evidence, the only hope we had was a confession. There's no lawyer on earth who's going to tell her to give us one of those."

The evidence! "I totally forgot. I have evidence."

Keith's head pops up and his shoulders square in an instant. "You're not kidding around, are you?"

"I couldn't. I wouldn't. Stay right here." In the blink of an eye, I dash down the stairs. But then I have to run back up and get the keys, then back down the stairs to open the bakery, retrieve the plastic bag and the mug, lock the bakery, and then back upstairs. "I have this!"

Keith twists in his chair and stares at the bag. "That looks like a mug from your bakery. Not too sure if I should be jumping for joy or checking to see if you have a fever?"

"Fever?" Confusion swirls around my features. "Right. I left out the best part. Myra was drinking out of this mug before she had the argument with me. Maybe it would have fingerprints."

He's out of the chair and across the room in a flash. Keith pulls the bag from my hand as though it contains a fragile egg. "You're sure? You saw her drink out of *this* mug?"

"Well, no."

His face slackens.

"I didn't see it. Jazz said Myra was drinking her coffee, then she saw me in the back, and she stormed in to have it out with me. When she stepped away, Myra set this mug down on the counter and never came back."

Keith slips one arm around me and squeezes. "I could kiss you, Cindy Claus."

Artikoa yips loudly, and my face heats like a glowing Yule Log.

At the same time, the color drains from Keith's face, and he recoils. "It's a— I would never — without your— Sorry. I need to get this down to the lab." He hurries out the door, and, less than a minute later, I hear his car roar to life on the street.

My overprotective arctic fox saunters toward me and tilts his wise head. "I may never be able to leave you alone again. He could kiss you?" Artikoa shakes his head. "He most certainly could not."

His concern evaporates in the heat that warms my heart. Keith kind of hugged me and said something about a kiss. I've never been kissed by anyone — except on the cheek by Mama and Papa. What if I don't know how to do it right? Curling elf boots! This doesn't sound like something I can talk to Jasmine about.

Guess I'll have to cross my fingers and hope for the best.

The *best* would be . . . if it happens.

CHAPTER 18

The following morning, after a restless night flopping between lovely visions of Keith and dark twisting nightmares, I drag myself down to the bakery. Before long, the hum of Christmas carols and the aroma of fresh-baked treats lift my spirit and re-energize my body.

A momentary disturbance on the retail side of the bakery pulls me from my happy place. I'm sure it's nothing Jasmine can't handle. So I pick up my shaker of hand-blended spices and cover the rectangle of buttered cinnamon roll dough with a generous sprinkling.

The unwelcome wild swaths of hair and broad shoulders of Myra Patara darken my doorway. Her low voice has a feral quality. "I was willing to take this building and simply watch you rot in prison for a crime you didn't commit."

The shaker falls from my hand as I gasp. "You? You stole the pan and planted my fingerprints?"

"It's not stealing if you leave it behind. I dropped it on the sidewalk when I was done." Wicked, guttural laughter rumbles from the woman.

Taking a deep breath for courage, I press on. "Well, it didn't work. The authorities know the prints were planted."

"If at first you don't succeed, try, try again, I always say." Her nostrils flare. "Although, the stakes are slightly higher now, Claus."

A chill races across my skin, and I'm certain Connie's ghost is the force inching the rolling pin within my reach. As I let my fingers circle around the familiar larchwood, a haunting howl echoes from the coffered ceiling.

So many things happen at once, my brain flips into massive overload!

As my hand tightens, time in the human world stands still.

Myra Patara transforms into something unholy — something supernatural. Twisting horns sprout from her head, and her face melts into a creature of nightmares. Her broad shoulders are covered with dirty, matted fur, and suddenly the image from my goth sweater has come to life.

"Krampus!?"

She snarls and takes a threatening step toward me.

Before her cloven hoof can hit the ground, a force to be reckoned with bowls into her back and sends her skittering across the hard floor of the bakery.

My mother told me bedtime stories about a race of shapeshifters that protected our polar realm, but I'd never seen one with my own eyes. Now, one of these mythical creatures is here — in the flesh. Or is it fur?

Standing before me is ten feet of imposing — I can't remember the word!

YETI. The name of legend pops into my head, and yet there's more. Something familiar about the energy, something almost *venerable*.

"Arti?"

Before the white beast can answer, Krampus climbs to her mismatched feet, one cloven hoof and one semi-human foot, and charges.

The yeti responds to the attack with a crushing blow of its gargantuan fist. The two titans are locked in what is certainly mortal combat.

As I watch, each movement of the powerful

snow creature confirms my suspicion. Artikoa is somehow part of this monstrous arctic protector.

The yeti folds Krampus into its deadly embrace — squeezing and twisting. I have to look away. I can't watch what my heart tells me is about to happen.

The evil monster screams of wickedness and vengeance.

A roar of retribution resounds. Then comes a flash of light so bright it temporarily blinds me.

When I pick myself up from the floor and blink away the radiating spots of light in my eyes, the second hand on the clock begins to move.

A small arctic fox sits peacefully opposite my baking table. "Cynthia, did she touch you?"

Dropping the rolling pin still clutched in my left hand, I take a deep breath and look myself over. "No. What happened? Was that— How did—?"

Artikoa's amber eyes shine brightly, yet there's a clear residue of worry.

The Krampus that attacked me has vanished. "Is that thing gone? Did you—?" A shudder passes over me. "You saved my life, Arti."

My most venerable elder lowers his pointed nose, briefly locks eyes with me, and bolts from the bakery.

Staggering to the front room, I struggle to

calm my racing heart. Jasmine is unharmed. A sigh of relief escapes.

"Cindy, is everything all right? There was a woman shouting for you. I thought she walked back here, but she must've bounced. I don't see her anywhere."

Carefully tiptoeing my way between the truth and a lie, I gaze warmly at Jasmine. "Yeah, she must be gone. Thanks, Jazz. Did she say what she wanted?"

"Nope. I offered her some coffee, but she, like, vanished. Supes weird. Right?"

"It definitely is. I better call Keith."

Jasmine bites her lip and bobs her chin. "Yup. Not that you need a reason — but totes."

Taking a deep breath as I lift the receiver from the cradle, my fingers tap out the now familiar number. "Hi. It's Cindy. There was an incident at— I don't know how to explain it. Can you come to the bakery?"

After placing the receiver in the cradle, I retrieve my larchwood rolling pin from the floor and give it a good scrub. The chill in the air has vanished. "Connie, if that was you trying to protect me. Thanks."

Silence.

As I wander into the retail area, I can't help but double down on my wish that Mama comes up with some way for me to communicate with ghosts.

Jasmine brews me a cup of chamomile tea, and I'm halfway through sipping the calming elixir when Keith arrives.

"What happened? Are you okay?" His shoulders are tense and his voice has a hard edge.

Swallowing, I gather my courage and motion for Keith to follow me into the back room. He looks around at the intense damage and shakes his head.

There's a large dent in my metal worktable, several holes in the wall, and even two bricks missing from the thick wall facing the alley.

"What the heck happened?"

"Myra. Myra Patara was here."

Keith's brow knits together as he slowly surveys the room. "One woman did this? This looks like a brawl in a biker bar or a grizzly bear attack."

I'm afraid to speak. Keith's theory is a little too close to the truth.

"Wait . . ." His face twists with confusion. "She was in a holding cell, waiting for her lawyer." He pulls out his mobile phone. "Winters here. Check holding."

There's an uncomfortable pause while he waits for confirmation of what he believes.

"What? When?" Keith exhales with muffled

rage and shoves his phone back into his pocket. "Chrisp says there's a hole in the back of the detention cell the size of a moose." He shakes his head. "Someone must've blown it up or smashed a truck—" His arms wave wildly.

"Yeah. That must be what happened." There's nothing else I can say without lying.

Keith stops and looks me over from head to toe. "You don't have a scratch on you." He crosses his arms and tilts his head.

"I ducked behind the table." My voice squeaks with a total lack of conviction. The words are a thin version of truth.

"Cindy, I'm trained to examine evidence and create a hypothesis about crime scenes. This doesn't make any sense. How could Myra Patara come back here and do this amount of damage to your bakery while you're unscathed?"

The way he's looking at me makes me uncomfortable. Earlier, he put his arm around me. He said he could kiss me. Now he's looking at me like I'm a suspect — or worse — a liar. Well, I can't lie, but I can't tell the truth either.

"Arti was here. He defended me." My gaze falls to the floor.

"That little *dog*, Cindy? That's almost more unbelievable." His jaw tightens. "Where's Myra

Patara? You're not going to tell me she walked away from this, are you?"

At least this question I can answer honestly. "I don't know. I looked away. I— When it was over, I looked back and it was just Artikoa sitting in the middle of the floor. She was— I don't know what happened to her."

Keith chews his bottom lip and shakes his head. "Nothing's adding up here, Cindy. But if Ms. Patara is responsible for this, then she's more dangerous than we ever imagined." He takes a steadying breath. "By the way, that was her print on the rolling pin holder from Ronnie's house. Thanks to your quick thinking with that coffee mug, we were able to pull a match."

"Oh, good." Wringing my hands, I still can't look Keith in the eyes.

"Yeah, I suppose it's good. She's responsible for killing Ronnie, and who knows what she would've done to you if Artikoa hadn't come to your rescue."

"I hope Connie will be relieved to know you found the killer." My eyes widen and I bite my tongue a second too late.

"Connie?" Keith shrugs. "I'm sure you meant Ronnie. I'm hoping he'll rest easier now, too."

The best I can muster is, "Mmhmm."

He casts his gaze around the back room one last time. "I'll write up a report and try to make as much sense of this as I possibly can. We'll put out a BOLO for Myra Patara — and a warrant for her arrest."

"Thank you." There's so much I want to say, but the fewer words, the better — for now.

Keith exhales slowly and, finally, relief lifts one side of his mouth. "Not for the first time, I'm glad I sleep across the hall from you. I'll leave my door open tonight just in case she decides to come back."

As the rest of his features soften, Keith steps closer. "I'm really glad you're okay, Cindy. I promised Artikoa a bone from the butchers. Looks like I'd better make that a whole T-bone steak, eh?"

I'm sure Arti would prefer a rabbit, but I won't ruin this moment with that fact. Chuckling, I look into his deep-green eyes. "Yeah, you better. He definitely saved my hide. Papa will be proud."

He reaches out and scoops up my hand with two fingers. "Am I gonna get an opportunity to meet your parents?"

The color drains from my face so quickly that I feel lightheaded and have to brace myself on the metal table.

"Oh! Hey! Easy, girl. I wasn't trying to— I didn't mean it like that."

Air rushes into my lungs. "No. It's okay. It's—Yeah, I don't know."

Keith laughs, drops my hand, and steps back. "You're one heck of a Christmas conundrum, Cindy. I better get back to the station and take care of this paperwork. Your bakery is closed for the next two days, right?"

"Is today the 23rd?"

"Yeah, why?"

"The funeral service!" Glancing at the clock, panic crushes my chest. "I have less than a half-hour to make myself presentable and get down to the funeral parlor. I've gotta go!"

"You always look great. I'll catch up with you tonight. I have a surprise—"

Keith's voice fades into the background as I take the stairs two at a time. Did he say surprise?

CHAPTER 19

The funeral proves a strange and disorienting experience. I can't say I'll be attending any more in the future. When I return to the bakery, I distract myself helping Jasmine fulfill all the customer orders for holiday treats. As the day draws to a close, exhaustion hits me like a frozen snowball.

"Why don't you head home, Jazz."

"I gotta sweep and stuff, boss."

"Nah. Leave it. There's a one hundred percent chance I'll be down here tomorrow or the next day. I'll handle the cleanup." Reaching into the register, I pull out several pieces of the green-and-white paper. "Here. You deserve a Christmas bonus. I couldn't run this place without you."

Jasmine accepts the wad of money and wipes away a happy tear. "Thanks, Cindy. I'm super pumped to work for you."

Next thing I know, she throws her arms around me and hugs me like a sister. "Merry Christmas, boss. Sorry, I didn't get anything for you."

"Merry Christmas, Jasmine." Leaning back, I let the joy of the season beam from my face. "All I want is snow! I love a white Christmas."

She laughs. "I can't do much about the weather, but maybe the big guy will grant your wish."

"The big guy?" My eyebrows lift.

"Yeah. You know. Santa." She winks and pulls off her apron.

As soon as she leaves, I trudge upstairs to fall into bed.

Artikoa is nowhere to be found, and Keith's apartment is silent.

Sleep will be my only friend. Sounds wonderful!

AS PREDICTED, MORNING FINDS ME IN THE BAKERY. I've put up the chairs, swept the floor, and cleaned the pastry case. Now, I'm stirring up a batch of peppermint hot chocolate while I wait for the cookies to cool enough to push the chocolate Santas into the centers.

A knock on the outer door pulls me from the back room.

"Keith!" Swinging open the door, my heart swells.

His expression reflects my happiness. "Wanted to let you know I pushed a package through the dog door for Artikoa. Is he in the apartment?"

"He is. Came home in the middle of the night. Little scamp. Thank you for keeping your promise to him. He'll be thrilled with your gift."

Keith sniffs the air like a wild animal. "Why don't you grab some of those Santa's Surprise cookies to go? I'd like to take you on a little adventure."

My heart nearly jumps out of my chest. I had forgotten to ask Jasmine about the details, but this definitely feels like another date. "Where are we going?"

"Kinda wanted to keep it a surprise, if that's okay with you." He tilts his head like a mischievous puppy. "Just grab a warm jacket, hat, and gloves. And don't forget those cookies."

As I pack cookies in a small green bakery box, the merriment of my little creations touches my face. Perhaps I'm talking to myself, or maybe Keith. Either way, I probably shouldn't have said this out loud. "I call these cookies Santa's Surprise Peanut Butter Cookies because my papa loves to grab these little babies hot from the oven, and he leaves thumbprints all over everything. Also, I replaced the normal chocolate drop candies with miniature chocolate Santa Clauses — in his honor."

As I close the flaps, I catch sight of Keith. His face is frozen in an expression that falls somewhere between concern and humor.

The color drains from my cheeks. My throat is dry. "Isn't that the funniest little story? People always ask me about the inspiration for my cookies. I have to say something." Technically, it's not a lie, but my voice is higher than normal, and I'm speaking so rapidly that I'm tripping over my tongue.

Relief echoes through Keith's laughter. "Welp, you really had me going for a minute there, Cindy. That's a fantastic story, by the way."

Grabbing the package of warm cookies, I hand the little box to Keith. "I'll run up to my apartment to grab my coat. Be right back."

My hands are shaking and a little bit sweaty. I drop the key on the floor outside the door, and Artikoa yips with concern.

"Don't worry. It's only me, Arti. I need to grab my coat."

When I enter the apartment, he drops his special treat and paces more like a mother fox protecting her kit than a trusted advisor. "Where are you going at this time of the morning? You said you'd be in the bakery until midday."

"Oh, no big deal. Keith is taking me on an adventure."

Artikoa stops. He is utterly motionless. In that way only a wild predator can be.

"What? He's a friend."

"How many friends have I found in your apartment at one in the morning?"

"Not many. I don't have that many friends. Plus, there's nothing to worry about. It's Christmas Eve, and I want to see the glistening treetops, not be stuck indoors all day!"

The snow-white fox plants himself firmly in front of the door. "I won't allow it. You have no experience in human relationships. You may not understand his intentions."

"His intentions? You sound like Mama."

"Your mother is a wise queen and knows the dangers of unpredictable human emotions." Artikoa's tail lowers and his hackles rise.

Despite my tingling anticipation, I keep my voice even. "I'll be safe with Keith. He's a good person, and you know he's on the Nice List."

At the mention of lists, the fox's sharp little ears perk up. "So, you continue to get information when you interact with people. Interesting. Your father will be pleased to hear that."

While Arti's distracted by his plans to make a report, I grab my warm coat and rush toward the door.

"Be back before dark, or I shall be forced to follow your scent to wherever Mr. Winters has taken you. And I will *speak* to him about his behavior." He yips once and returns to the butcher's treat from Keith.

No part of that seems like an empty threat. If Arti were to reveal his ability to speak actual English, my opportunity to pass myself off as a twenty-something human figure would be over in a heartbeat.

Bowing as I exit, I do not try to disagree with this ancient creature.

Keith waits at the bottom of the steps and angles his head back as I descend. "You look worried. We don't have to go if you don't want to." He shifts his weight from one foot to the other, and I can sense his disappointment.

"Oh no. I had a little disagreement with Artikoa, but—" Icebergs! Humans don't argue with their animals. Do they?

Keith laughs out loud. "I know exactly what you mean. I had an English bulldog that could definitely hold his own in extemporaneous debate." He reaches a hand toward me, and I place mine in his without thinking.

Heat crackles up my arm faster than chestnuts roasting over an open fire. "Thanks."

He glances at the floor as he grins. "My car's right outside."

As we drive toward our mysterious destination, Keith shares what he knows about our lovely little town. "It's my understanding that the town was founded by Vikings. Legend has it they battled their way across what's now Canada, from Newfoundland, gathering supplies and probably women — sorry about that part — when they found this little area."

"They found Silver Shoals?" I silently wonder if my father knew any Vikings?

My tour guide smiles warmly. "It wasn't Silver Shoals back then. It wasn't anything. They probably chose the area because of the topography. The hillside gives a good vantage point for anyone approaching from the great lake, and the shallow shoals would have given any boats they constructed a clear advantage."

"Why?"

"Viking ships were narrow and had shallow drafts, which means they could easily travel in much shallower water than their European counterparts." His excitement is contagious.

"So this town used to be a Viking outpost?"

"That's right. A lot of the families around here can trace their lineage back to those original settlers. In fact, the place I'm taking you is one of the oldest structures in the area."

Excitement pulses through my veins as Keith drives to the mysterious destination. As we crest the hill we've been climbing, a great stone tower stands out starkly against the grey-white winter sky.

"What is that?"

"That is Ivarsson Tower." Keith maneuvers his car into a spot next to a bare-limbed oak. "We park here and walk up the rest of the way."

When I hop out of the car, Keith shakes his head. "I would've gotten the door for you, Cindy."

"Oh, it's no problem. I know how to open doors."

His chin drops to his chest as he shrugs.

If I weren't so upset with Artikoa, I'd probably ask the nosey fox what I did wrong when I get home. Not today.

Keith leads the way to some stone steps cut into the earth below the tower. The wind howls across the hillside, and my hair is whipping in my eyes like a wild creature with a mind of its own.

Scraping it all back, I search the pocket of my green wool coat for a hair tie. Thank goodness!

After fighting my whirlwind of hair, I manage to secure most of it and restore a clear line of sight between myself and Keith.

He motions for me to join him inside the tower.

"Is it safe? You said it was really old, right?"

"Very. The Vikings were warriors and conquerors. They feared retaliation. Before they even built dwellings for themselves, they built this lookout tower to claim the land. Even the name served as a warning. Ivarsson means warrior or army. They used local granite stone and hydraulic lime to create this marvel. Archaeologists estimate the structure originated in the 1300s."

"Wow, that's before my papa—" Biting my lip, I pretend to choke on an errant hair that's gotten in my mouth. I was about to say that was before Santa expanded his toy delivery to the North American continent, but luckily I caught myself. I quickly change the subject. "Can we climb the stairs?"

"You betcha." Keith leads the way up the short flight of steps that takes us to the second floor of the tower.

Each floor of the large circular tower has six windows, edged in smaller stone, around the circumference. A flight of eight thick steps leads to the next level. There are six levels in all. When we reach the highest point of the tower, the view is stunning. Blessed with elven sight, I can see miles farther than an average human. However, I know better than to make that public.

"It's stunning. The lake is frozen as far as the eye can see. The Vikings must've come during the summer."

"Possibly. They may have had an advance party that came on foot, or maybe they stole some sled dogs from one of the villages they plundered. Either way, they eventually arrived here and settled. Then they built boats for fishing and larger vessels for protection."

"I wish I could've seen that." I'd love to tell Keith I've never been on a boat, but I don't want to give him any reason for concern.

His cheeks are pink from the cold, but his grin is electric. "This summer, I'll take you out to Erikson Island. We can rent a glass-bottom boat for a couple hours. There's a sunken Viking ship we could glide over. It's pretty great."

Keith's excitement is palpable. It feels like a child opening exactly what they wanted for Christmas. I enjoy being in the presence of his bliss. It's nice to know there's more to him than solving murders.

A dastardly wind knifes through the tower and my teeth chatter.

Keith steps closer and places an arm around my shoulders. "We should get going. You look chilled to the bone."

Now is definitely not the time to let him know that a girl from the North Pole can tolerate temperatures far more severe than this. Instead, now is the time to enjoy that arm wrapped around my shoulders.

"No rush. The view really is breathtaking."

Of course, that's not the only thing taking my breath away.

As I turn, Keith leans in and his warm lips meet mine. A sparkle like Christmas twinkle lights zips through my tummy.

"Merry Christmas, Cindy." His breath forms a cloud.

"Merry—"

Before I can finish my reply, he tips his head down and I press my lips to his.

I definitely won't be telling Artikoa about this early holiday gift!

CHAPTER 20

My Christmas Eve date with Keith was a marvelous success. By the time I get home and hang my stocking, I can barely keep my eyes open. Setting out a plate of Santa's Surprise Peanut Butter Cookies and a big mug of peppermint hot chocolate, I crawl into bed.

Even as my head hits the pillow, I know I'll never stay awake long enough to see my father arrive.

I'm dreaming of a white Christmas, with beautiful snowflakes covering everything in Silver Shoals, when a familiar voice calls out.

"Marshmallow. Time to wake up, Marshmallow."

"Papa!"

When I leap from my bed, strong arms encircle me, and the feeling of safety and home envelops me. My father pats my back.

"Thank you for the cookies."

As I lift my head from his red velvet coat, I catch a flicker of glistening snowflakes out the window. "Is it snowing?"

His warm belly laugh fills my tiny apartment. "I heard my princess wanted a white Christmas. That's the best I can do, dear."

"It's perfect, Papa. Just like the ones I used to enjoy at the North Pole. You always know what I want."

"I do." He chuckles and takes a seat in the plush green-velvet chair. As he nibbles on his cookies and peppermint cocoa, he glances toward Artikoa. "Greetings, my most trusted advisor."

Artikoa bows his head respectfully. "The children will be pleased to hear your sleigh bells in the snow this evening, sir."

Before Artikoa can tattle, I tell Papa about the wild events following Ronnie's death. When we get to the final battle in the bakery, I glance toward the arctic elder. "Do you want to tell this part?"

Oddly, he lowers his gaze and offers only a subtle shake of the head.

"Okay, I'll tell it." My heart races with fresh adrenaline as I tell my father the amazing heroics of Artikoa, most venerable elder and secret yeti. "He battled Krampus and— I'm not sure what happened to it, but it's no longer in this world. Arti saved my life. The elves should write a song about him, Papa."

When I finish, my father sets down his empty plate and wipes a swollen tear from the corner of his eye.

"This was always one of my fears, Marshmallow. Your mother and I didn't keep you at the North Pole on a whim. You were correct in assuming that Myra Patara was a krampus. Unfortunately, she's not the only one of her kind. Centuries ago, the first krampus, my cousin and I—"

"We're related to the krampus?" There's a tidbit Mama left out of my bedtime stories.

"To everything, there is a yin and a yang. Light and shadow. Good and evil. There cannot be a St. Nicholas without the krampus." His expression is weary, and a hint of regret hangs in the air. "In the beginning, we worked together. I would make the List, recording all the good boys and girls. Krampus would visit bad boys and girls — punishing them with a switch made of birch twigs — and that was that. But, as time passed, the descendants of my cousin became darker." My father crosses his hands over his large belly and exhales sadness.

"They don't have long lives like you and Mama?"

"No, my dear. Darkness rotted away at their soul. And eventually, the darkness became too heavy. The krampus creatures began to take the bad boys and girls, perhaps eating them, perhaps banishing them to Siberia. When rumors of boys and girls being dragged to hell's doorstep came to my attention, I terminated my agreement with the krampus."

I've never seen my father truly angry before. The expression hardening his features sends a shock of fear racing across my skin.

"Without access to my List they're helpless to identify the naughty children. Eventually they wandered into the wilderness, haunting various dark and ancient forests." His sigh carries the weight of ages. "Your mother and I were safe in a protected village in the North Pole. When you chose to leave—"

"I didn't know the whole story, Papa. I never would've left. I'm so sorry!"

"There's no need to apologize, my dear sweet little Marshmallow. Artikoa has permanently dispatched this krampus. Now that your mother and I know they have identified you, we will be vigilant."

Artikoa clears his throat, but refrains from speaking.

Santa turns toward the wise fox and bows. "My faith in you has not wavered. There is no creature on earth or in the heavens above that is better suited to watch over my daughter than you, old friend."

"It is my honor." Artikoa lifts his nose, and his orange-yellow eyes blaze. "No harm will come to the heir on my watch, sir."

A respectful silence hangs in the air, but my guilt won't fade. "Papa, if you think I should return—"

"As I said earlier, I always know what you need. You need this independence to follow the thing that you love, as much as I followed my passion for toys to make children happy. You love what you do, and this bakery is an extension of you. You're sharing your passion and making other people happy. I couldn't possibly ask you to abandon that."

"Thank you, Papa." I hadn't realized how I'd pinched my shoulders together, expecting the worst. Relief floods through me.

"Now we know the old feud still burns. This krampus seemed intent on destroying your livelihood by taking the building. She only came after you personally when the sale was in jeopardy. Your mother will know what to do." Once again, he gazes at the most venerable elder. "Of course, Artikoa is master of all he surveys. He will protect you, and our kingdom will inform its network of wild creatures to be more on guard. Next time, they will not dare set foot in your bakery, my dear."

His loving hand reaches across and squeezes mine. "I'm so glad you're safe. Now, are you ready for your present?"

"Almost." Leaping from my chair, I creak open my traveling trunk and root around. "Aha! I made this for Mama. Can you deliver it?"

Papa reaches out and accepts the ristra with a proud grin. "These are your mother's favorite chiles! Where did you get this?"

"I made it, Papa. Do you think she'll like it?" My heart races with concern.

His "ho, ho, ho" laughter lights up the room as he secures the string of dried chile peppers in his bag. "The queen will be pleased beyond measure." He presses a hand to the side of his mouth and whispers conspiratorially, "Plus, you saved me a stop, Marshmallow. After I make my last delivery, I'll be able to fly straight home and skip picking up this special spice for your mother."

"Does that count as a present for you, Papa?" I can hardly keep a straight face.

Another round of laughter brings a tear of joy

to his eye. "That reminds me, your mother said she's working on the ghost ritual — whatever that means. She will contact you when she has all the details sorted."

"Tell her thank you. I hope she likes her present." A nervous flush touches my cheeks.

"I know she will, Marshmallow. Now for yours."

I feel like a fifty-five-year-old elf as the joy of anticipating Santa's present floods through me. "Wow. I thought the snow was my present. And that was amazing and wonderful. But there's more?"

"There is indeed more." Santa makes a huge ruckus digging through his sack, and eventually pulls out a golden envelope with an intricate red wax seal.

Years of training kick in to keep my smile bright, even though an envelope was not what I had hoped for. Carefully loosening the wax seal, I open the gilt flap and extract a thick packet of papers.

"These look like legal documents. What is it, Papa?"

"It's the deed to this building, my sweet Cherubim."

"How did— Sven said Myra—"

"You should know better than to ask Santa his secrets, my child."

Wheels are spinning inside my head, and I feel as though it's the final push at the toy factory. "So I own the bakery?"

"The entire building. And I paid Sven handsomely for it." He rubs his round belly and chuckles. "Well, the elf acting as my real estate agent paid him handsomely. Mr. Tollesson's six children will have an especially wonderful Christmas this year."

Leaping from my chair, the papers flutter to the ground as I throw my arms around my father's neck and let my tears fall into his fluffy white beard.

"Thank you, Papa. I know I say it every year, but this is truly the best Christmas ever!"

He hugs me tight. "May your days be merry and bright, Marshmallow."

RECIPE: HOLIDAY
APPLE DUMPLINGS

Holiday Apple Dumplings

Yield: 6 dumplings
Ingredients
<u>For the dough:</u>

- 3 cups (375 grams) **unbleached flour**
- 1 teaspoon (6 grams) **salt**
- ½ teaspoon (3 grams) ground **cinnamon**
- ½ teaspoon (3 grams) ground **nutmeg**
- ¼ teaspoon (2 grams) ground **clove**
- 1 cup (216 grams) **butter**, *chilled and cut into small pieces*

- 2 Tablespoons (30 ml) of apple cider vinegar
- ½ cup (118 ml) **iced water**

For the filling:

- 3 Tablespoons (54 grams) **butter**, cut into six ½-Tablespoon (9 grams) chunks
- 6 pitted **prunes**, diced small
- 6 dried **apricots**, diced small
- 2½ Tablespoons (30 grams) dried **cranberries**

Additional Ingredients:

6 medium-sized **Granny Smith apples,** peeled and cored (substitute your favorite)

1 **egg**, beaten to glaze the pastry-wrapped apples

Instructions
Make the filling:

1. Dice prunes and apricots. Mix with cranberries. Set aside.
2. Butter cubes will be pushed into cored apples, on top of fruit filling.

Make the dough:

1. Pulse flour, spices, and salt in a food processor to combine. Add butter and pulse until mixture resembles coarse breadcrumbs with pieces of butter still visible. About 25 pulses.
2. Combine vinegar and ½ cup iced water in a measuring cup. While pulsing, drizzle in vinegar mixture; pulse until dough comes together. Dough should be pliable, but not sticky. About 15 pulses.
3. Turn out dough and divide into 6 equal parts. Place each part on a sheet of plastic wrap and roll each part into approx. 8-inch square. Cover with another layer of plastic wrap and chill until firm, about 1 hour.
4. Peel and core the apples.
5. Preheat oven to 350°F/177°C. Line a large half-sheet baking pan with parchment paper or a silicone baking mat.
6. Remove dough squares from refrigerator. Place one prepared apple in the center of each dough square. Stuff each core with equal parts fruit filling and **one** ½-Tablespoon (9 grams) butter chunk.

7. Brush the edges of the dough square lightly with water. Bring the edges up around the apple and seal with additional water. Trim off excess.

8. *OPTION: Roll out trimmings and cut decorative leaves to decorate each dumpling.

9. Place each wrapped apple on parchment-covered baking tray. Glaze each apple with beaten egg.

10. Bake for 30–45 minutes, or until golden brown, and pierce easily with a sharp skewer.

SERVE: Serve hot with fresh whipped cream or ice cream and a cinnamon stick.

RECIPE: NORTH POLE GOOEY CARAMEL CINNAMON ROLLS

North Pole Gooey Caramel Cinnamon Rolls
(*with Connie's secret ingredient!*)

Yield: 36 rolls
Ingredients
Rolls

- 1½ cup (192 grams) raisins
- ½ cup (125 ml) dark rum (*Cindy added this from Connie's special recipe!*)
- 3 loaves frozen sweet or white bread dough, thawed but not doubled*
- ⅓ cup (75 ml) vegetable oil or melted butter**

- ⅔ cup (147 grams) packed brown sugar (you can substitute Sukrin Gold)
- 3 Tablespoon (43 grams) ground cinnamon
- ⅔ teaspoon (9.5 grams) ground nutmeg
- ½ teaspoon (7 grams) ground allspice

Topping

- 1 cup (191 grams) confectioner's sugar (you can substitute powdered erythritol - but I'm not a fan)
- 1 cup (191 grams) brown sugar (you can substitute Sukrin Gold)
- ⅔ cup (150 ml) heavy whipping cream**
- 1½ teaspoon (7.5 ml) vanilla
- 1⅓ cups (171 grams) coarsely chopped pecans***

Non-stick cooking spray for pans

Cindy's Tips & Tricks

*Using frozen loaves from your grocery store's freezer section is a time saver. If you're a baker like me and you have a favorite sweet bread recipe — use it!

**If you want to avoid dairy, use vegetable oil instead of butter and substitute thick, rich canned coconut cream for the heavy whipping cream. Oh, and stick with ALL brown sugar (2 cups [383 grams], no confectioner's) on the topping.

***If you're allergic to nuts, just leave out the pecans.

Instructions

1. In a small bowl, soak raisins in the dark rum (skip this step if you want to avoid the alcohol component). Cover and set aside. This can be done up to a week in advance.
2. Prepare the topping: In a mixing bowl, stir together sugars, whipping cream, and vanilla until blended.
3. Spray three 9 x 1½-inch (23 x 3.8 cm) round cake pans with non-stick cooking spray. Evenly divide the topping mixture into pans and sprinkle with chopped pecans, if desired. Set pans aside.
4. Prepare the rolls: On a floured surface, roll each loaf into a 12 x 8 x ¼-inch (31 x 20 x 0.64 cm) rectangle. Generously brush each sheet of dough with vegetable oil or melted butter.
5. In a small bowl, mix together brown sugar, cinnamon and nutmeg. Sprinkle

each sheet of dough with mix and top with rum-soaked raisins. **NOTE**: The raisins should've absorbed all the rum at this point. If there is too much liquid left — drain it off —do not add that to your dough, or your rolls will be soggy.

6. Roll up rectangles, jelly-roll style, starting along the 12-inch (31 cm) edge. Pinch dough to seal. Cut into 12 equal slices, roughly 1-inch (2.6 cm) thick.

7. Place rolls, spiral side down, in prepared cake pans. Cover with wax paper and then a towel; let rise in a warm place for 30 minutes or until doubled in size.

8. Preheat oven to 375°F/191°C. Bake uncovered for 25–30 minutes.

9. **NOTE**: The last 10 minutes of baking cover with foil to prevent over-browning.

10. Cool in pans for 8 minutes. Invert onto a serving plate. Best warm. Makes 36 rolls.

RECIPE: SANTA'S SURPRISE PEANUT BUTTER COOKIES

Santa's Surprise Peanut Butter Cookies

Yield: 36 cookies
Ingredients
<u>For the cookies:</u>

- ½ cup (108 grams) **butter**, softened (you can substitute margarine)
- ½ cup (108 grams) **peanut butter**, creamy (you can substitute almond butter)
- ½ cup (100 grams) **granulated sugar** (you can substitute erythritol) + additional for rolling

- ½ cup (100 grams) **dark brown sugar** (you can substitute Sukrin Gold)
- 1 large **egg**, *room temperature*
- 1¾ cups (219 grams) **unbleached flour**
- ½ teaspoon (3 grams) **salt**
- 1 teaspoon (4.75 grams) **baking soda**
- 1 teaspoon (5 ml) **vanilla**

For the Surprise:

- 36 **Riegelein "MINIS" Chocolate Santas** (you can substitute Hershey's Kisses)

Instructions
Make the cookies:

1. Preheat oven to 375°F/191°C. Line a large half-sheet baking pan with parchment paper or a silicone baking mat.
2. In a medium mixing bowl, whisk together the flour, baking soda, and salt. Set aside.
3. Cream butter and both sugars together using a stand mixer fitted with the paddle attachment (or in a large mixing

bowl with a hand mixer) on medium speed until light and fluffy, about 2 minutes.

4. Add egg, peanut butter, and vanilla. Beat until incorporated.

5. Gradually add the dry ingredients and beat on low speed until combined (the dough should be stiff).

6. Use a small cookie scoop to scoop out 1 Tablespoon (14.3 grams) of cookie dough. Roll into 1-inch (2.6 cm) balls and then roll in additional granulated sugar (or erythritol). Drop on the prepared baking sheet, spaced 2 inches (5 cm) apart.

7. Bake for 10–12 minutes until edges are lightly brown.

8. Remove from oven and immediately press one chocolate Santa in the center of each warm cookie.

9. Allow cookies to cool on the cookie sheet for 3 minutes before carefully transferring to a wire cooling rack to cool completely.

How to store: Store cookies in an airtight container at room temperature for up to 4 days.

Store with parchment paper between layers to prevent the Santas from sticking.

How to freeze: If planning to make a large batch to freeze, place in single layers with sheets of parchment paper between. Store in airtight container in the freezer for up to 2 months.

RECIPE: CRANBERRY-ORANGE YULETIDE SCONES

Cranberry-Orange Yuletide Scones

Yield: 8 scones
Ingredients

- 3 cups (375 grams) **all-purpose flour**
- 1 Tablespoon (14.3 grams) **baking powder** (*Make sure it's fresh!*)
- ½ teaspoon (3 grams) **salt**
- ½ cup (100 grams) **granulated sugar** (you can substitute erythritol)
- ½ cup (108 grams) **unsalted cold butter**, cut into cubes
- ½ cup (120 ml) cold **buttermilk**
- ¼ cup (60 ml) cold **sour cream**

- 1 Tablespoon (15 ml) **vanilla extract**
- ½ teaspoon (2.5 ml) **almond extract**
- 1 Tablespoon (14.3 grams) freshly grated **orange zest**
- ¾ cup (96 grams) dried or frozen **cranberries**, roughly chopped (*If you use frozen, be sure to thaw and drain!*)

For the Heavy Cream Wash:

- ¼ cup (60 ml) **heavy cream** + 1 Tablespoon (15 ml) water

Orange Glaze:

- 1 cup (192 grams) **confectioner's sugar**
- 2–3 Tablespoons (30–45 ml) fresh-squeezed **orange juice**
- ¼ cup (57 grams) **red sparkling sugar**

Instructions

1. Preheat oven to 400°F/205°C. Place parchment paper on a large baking sheet or tray and set aside.
2. Combine flour, baking powder, salt, and sugar in a large mixing bowl.

3. Cut the cold butter into small cubes. Add the cold butter cubes to the bowl, and, using a pastry cutter, work the butter into the flour mixture until it resembles coarse meal (nothing larger than pea-size).
4. Whisk together the buttermilk, sour cream, vanilla extract, and almond extract.
5. Create a well in the center of the dry ingredients. Pour the buttermilk mixture into the center. Using a stiff rubber spatula, fold the mixture together a few times.
6. Pour the crumbly mixture out onto a lightly floured surface or silicone mat.
7. Next, add the orange zest and chopped cranberries.
8. Gently knead the dough to incorporate the add-ins. Do not overwork the dough. It should just be combined. Press it into a large circle about 2 inches/5 cm thick.
9. Using a pastry knife, cut dough into 8 wedges
10. Brush with heavy cream wash.
11. Place scones, "wash" side up, on the prepared baking sheet or tray.

12. Bake for 25–30 minutes, or until golden brown and cooked through.
13. Remove from oven and place scones on a wire rack to cool.
14. When cooled, drizzle with Orange Glaze and sprinkle with red sparkling sugar.

Storing Scones: Glazed or un-glazed scones can be kept at room temperature for 2 days or in the refrigerator for up to 5 days.

RECIPE: CHRISTMAS CARROT COOKIES

Christmas Carrot Cookies

Yield: 34 cookies
Ingredients
For the cookies:

- 1 cup (128 grams) peeled and finely shredded **carrots** (approx. 3 carrots), *you can steam and mash them if you prefer*
- 1 cup (200 grams) **granulated sugar** (you can substitute erythritol)
- ¾ cup (162 grams) **butter**, *softened to room temperature* (you can substitute shortening)

- 2 large **eggs**, *room temperature*
- 2 cups (250 grams) **unbleached flour**
- ½ teaspoon (3 grams) **salt**
- 2 teaspoons (9.5 grams) **baking powder**
- 1 teaspoon (5 ml) **vanilla**
- 1 teaspoon (4.8 grams) **orange zest** (zest the entire orange and reserve the rest for the icing)

For the icing:

- 2½ cups (479 grams) **confectioners' sugar** (run through a sifter if you want to ensure no lumps)
- ¼ cup (54 grams) **butter,** *softened to room temperature*
- 1½–2 Tablespoons (22–30 ml) **fresh squeezed juice of an orange**
- Remaining reserved **zest** of one orange

Instructions
Make the cookies:

1. Preheat oven to 375°F/191°C. Line a large half-sheet baking pan with parchment paper or a silicone baking mat.

2. In a medium mixing bowl, whisk together the flour, baking powder, and salt. Set aside.

3. Cream butter and sugar together using a stand mixer fitted with the paddle attachment (or in a large mixing bowl with a hand mixer) on medium speed until light and fluffy, about 2 minutes.

4. Add eggs, finely shredded carrots, vanilla and 1 teaspoon orange zest. Beat until incorporated.

5. Gradually add the dry ingredients and beat on low speed until combined (the dough will be sticky).

6. Use a small cookie scoop to scoop out 1 Tablespoon of cookie dough. Drop on the prepared baking sheet, spaced 2 inches apart.

7. Bake for 10–12 minutes until edges are lightly brown and center springs back. Allow cookies to cool on the cookie sheet for 5 minutes before carefully transferring to a wire cooling rack to cool completely.

Make the icing:

1. In a medium mixing bowl, beat the butter and zest until combined. Add confectioners' sugar and orange juice. Slowly mix until smooth. If the icing is too thick, add more orange juice, 1 teaspoon at a time, to thin it out.
2. Spread the icing on the cooled cookies with an offset spatula. Allow the icing to set before storing.

How to store: Store carrot cookies in an airtight container at room temperature for up to 4 days. Store in a single layer to prevent the icing from smudging. You could also store each cookie in a small cupcake liner so that they don't touch each other and cause the icing to smudge off on each other.

How to freeze: If planning to make a large batch to freeze, I would recommend icing them prior to freezing. This icing freezes well. Place in single layers in an airtight container with sheets of parchment paper between. Store in the freezer for up to 3 months.

End of Book 2

But, more mysteries await...

Curl up with another case from the Christmas Catastrophe Mysteries series!

A NOTE FROM TRIXIE

Feel free to celebrate the holidays with your friends and family — anytime of year! Thanks for being on the Nice List.

One of the best parts of bringing Cindy to life continues to be the wonderful feedback from early readers. Thank you to my alpha readers, Angel and Michael. HUGE thanks to my fantastic beta readers who give me extremely useful and honest feedback: Nadine Peterse-Vrijhof and Veronica McIntyre. And big hugs to the world's best ARC Team – Trixie's Mystery ARC Detectives!

Thank you to my thorough editor Philip Newey! I love the way his mind dissects a story. I'd also like to give heaps of gratitude to Roxx at Proof

Perfect for the much needed proofing! Any remaining errors are my own.

I love baking! When my grandmother passed, I was lucky enough to inherit her recipe box. What a treasure! It brings a smile to my face every time I'm able to share one of her special bakes with you.

FUN FACT: I've actually worked in a vegetarian restaurant as a cook!

My favorite line from this case: "Blizzards! That fox is pushing his enchanted luck." -Cindy

If you enjoyed this mystery, you can find more of my humorous paranormal cozies in the Mitzy Moon Mysteries, Harper and Moon Investigations, the Magical Renaissance Faire Mysteries, and the Mysteries of Moonlight Manor

We're so glad you chose to visit Silver Shoals. Stay tuned for another Christmas Catastrophe.

Trixie Silvertale (October 2024)

LINZER COOKIE MURDER

A shocking attack. A terrible truth. Will our unseasoned baker burn the wrong bridges?

Cindy Claus enjoys her successful bakery business. She's finally proven to be more than the heir to her father's sleigh. But right in the middle of her busiest season, a panicked message from her regal mother threatens to destroy her dreams.

With Santa hovering on death's doorstep and Cindy delivering the presents this year, she'll need her new sleuthing skills and the help of her father's trusted arctic fox to save Saint Nic. But without a major holiday miracle, this could be the beginning of the end...

Can Cindy corner the culprit, or will this be the world's last Christmas?

Linzer Cookie Murder is the third book in the festive paranormal cozy series, Christmas Catastrophe Mysteries. If you like kind-hearted heroines, furry sidekicks, and a dash of mistletoe magic, then you'll love Trixie Silvertale's Yuletide puzzler.

Buy *Linzer Cookie Murder* to wrap up a mystery today!

*Features recipes from Cindy's bakery!

Grab your next read here!
readerlinks.com/l/5211923

Scan this QR Code with the camera on your phone. You'll be taken right to the next Christmas Catastrophe Mysteries *adventure!*

SPECIAL INVITATION . . .

In between Christmas Catastrophe Mysteries, you can come visit Pin Cherry Harbor!

Get access to the Exclusive Mitzy Moon Mysteries character quiz – free!

Find out which character you are in Pin Cherry Harbor and see if you have what it takes to be part of Mitzy's gang.

This quiz is only available to members of the Paranormal Cozy Club, Trixie Silvertale's readers group.

Visit the link below to join the Trixie's Club and get access to the quiz:

http://trixiesilvertale.com/paranormal-cozy-club/

Once you're in the Club, you'll also be the first to receive updates from Pin Cherry Harbor and access to giveaways, new release announcements, behind-the-scenes secrets, and much more!

Scan this QR Code with the camera on your phone. You'll be taken right to the page to join the Club!

THANK YOU!

Trying out a new book is always a risk and I'm thankful that you rolled the dice with Cindy Claus. If you loved the book, the sweetest thing you can do (*even sweeter than peppermint hot chocolate*) is to leave a review so that other readers will take a chance on Cindy and Artikoa.

Don't feel you have to write a book report. A brief comment like, "Can't wait to read the next book in this series!" will help potential readers make their choice.

Leave a quick review HERE
https://readerlinks.com/l/4041381

THANK YOU!

Thank you kindly, and I'll see you in Silver Shoals!

ALSO BY TRIXIE SILVERTALE

Mitzy Moon Mysteries

Fries and Alibis: Paranormal Cozy Mystery

Tattoos and Clues: Paranormal Cozy Mystery

Wings and Broken Things: Paranormal Cozy Mystery

Sparks and Landmarks: Paranormal Cozy Mystery

Charms and Firearms: Paranormal Cozy Mystery

Bars and Boxcars: Paranormal Cozy Mystery

Swords and Fallen Lords: Paranormal Cozy Mystery

Wakes and High Stakes: Paranormal Cozy Mystery

Tracks and Flashbacks: Paranormal Cozy Mystery

Lies and Pumpkin Pies: Paranormal Cozy Mystery

Hopes and Slippery Slopes: Paranormal Cozy Mystery

Hearts and Dark Arts: Paranormal Cozy Mystery

Dames and Deadly Games: Paranormal Cozy Mystery

Castaways and Longer Days: Paranormal Cozy Mystery

Schemes and Bad Dreams: Paranormal Cozy Mystery

Carols and Yule Perils: Paranormal Cozy Mystery

Dangers and Empty Mangers: Paranormal Cozy Mystery

Heists and Poltergeists: Paranormal Cozy Mystery

Blades and Bridesmaids: Paranormal Cozy Mystery

Scones and Tombstones: Paranormal Cozy Mystery

Vandals and Yule Scandals: Paranormal Cozy Mystery

Harper and Moon Investigations

Ropes and Last Hopes: Paranormal Cozy Mystery

Bells and Bombshells: Paranormal Cozy Mystery

Rodeo Clowns and Shakedowns: Paranormal Cozy Mystery

Stiffs and Petroglyphs: Paranormal Cozy Mystery

Fatal Wines and Valentines: Paranormal Cozy Mystery

April Curses and May Hearses: Paranormal Cozy Mystery

Wheels and Dirty Deals: Paranormal Cozy Mystery

Scripts and Empty Crypts: Paranormal Cozy Mystery

Christmas Catastrophe Mysteries

Peppermint Cookie Murder: Paranormal Cozy Mystery

Apple Dumpling Murder: Paranormal Cozy Mystery

Linzer Cookie Murder: Paranormal Cozy Mystery

Chocolate Crinkle Cookie Murder: Paranormal Cozy Mystery

...more to come!

MAGICAL RENAISSANCE
FAIRE MYSTERIES

Explore the world of Coriander the Conjurer. A fortune-telling fairy with a heart of gold!

Book 1:

All Swell That Ends Spell – A dubious festival. A fatal swim. Can this fortune-telling fairy herald the true killer?

Book 2:

Fairy Wives of Windsor – A jolly Faire. A shocking murder. Can this furtive fairy outsmart the killer?

Book 3:

Double Double Royal Trouble – When a treat-peddling witch is found dead, will this cursed faire crumble?

MYSTERIES OF
MOONLIGHT MANOR

Join Sydney Coleman and her unruly ghosts, as they solve mysteries in a truly haunted mansion!

Book 1: **Moonlight and Mischief** – She's desperate for a fresh start, but is a mansion on sale too good to be true?

Book 2: **Moonlight and Magic** – A haunted Halloween tour seem like the perfect plan, until there's murder...

Book 3: **Moonlight and Mayhem** – An unwelcome visitor. A surprising past. Will her fire sale end in smoke?

ABOUT THE AUTHOR

USA TODAY Bestselling author Trixie Silvertale grew up reading an endless supply of Lilian Jackson Braun, Hardy Boys, and Nancy Drew novels. She loves the amateur sleuths in cozy mysteries and obsesses about all things paranormal. Those two passions unite in all her paranormal cozy mysteries, and she's thrilled to write them and share them with you.

When she's not consumed by writing, she bakes to fuel her creative engine and pulls weeds in her herb garden to clear her head (*and sometimes she pulls out her hair, but mostly weeds*).

Greetings are welcome:
trixie@trixiesilvertale.com

 facebook.com/TrixieSilvertale
 instagram.com/trixiesilvertale
 bookbub.com/authors/trixie-silvertale